The Case of the Jaded Jack Russell

A Thousand Islands Doggy Inn Mystery

B.R. Snow

I0628422

Copyright © 2017 B.R. Snow

ISBN: 978-1-942691-32-7

Website: www.brsnow.net/

Twitter: @BernSnow

Facebook: facebook.com/bernsnow

Cover Design: Reggie Cullen

Cover Photo: James R. Miller

Other Books by B.R. Snow

The Thousand Islands Doggy Inn Mysteries

- The Case of the Abandoned Aussie
- The Case of the Brokenhearted Bulldog
- The Case of the Caged Cockers
- The Case of the Dapper Dandie Dinmont
- The Case of the Eccentric Elkhound
- The Case of the Faithful Frenchie
- The Case of the Graceful Goldens
- The Case of the Hurricane Hounds
- The Case of the Itinerant Ibizan

The Whiskey Run Chronicles

- Episode 1 – The Dry Season Approaches
- Episode 2 – Friends and Enemies
- Episode 3 – Let the Games Begin
- Episode 4 – Enter the Revenuer
- Episode 5 – A Changing Landscape
- Episode 6 – Entrepreneurial Spirits
- Episode 7 – All Hands On Deck
- The Whiskey Run Chronicles – The Complete Volume 1

The Damaged Posse

- American Midnight
- Larrikin Gene
- Sneaker World
- Summerman
- The Duplicates

Other Books

- Divorce Hotel
- Either Ore

To Laurie

Chapter 1

I pulled to a stop in front of the Chateau Lavalier, lowered the driver side window, and smiled at the uniformed man standing next to the car. He opened the door, held it as a gust of wind threatened to slam it shut, and waited patiently for me to get out.

"Welcome to the Chateau Lavalier."

"Thank you. It's nice to be here. We've heard a lot of good things about this hotel."

"And all of them are true," he said with a slight bow. "Are you here for the conference?"

"The Animal Entrepreneurs Expo," I said, reaching into the back seat for my bag and groaning when my back protested. "I really need to get to the gym."

"What's that?"

"Nothing."

"Are you okay? It sounded like you might have pulled something. Like the lower half of your body."

"Funny. I'm fine," I said, grimacing as I settled back into the driver seat to wait out the spasm.

"Maybe you should stretch a bit when you get out. Long car rides can be tough on the back," he said, still holding the door open, but glancing back at the line of cars that was beginning to form behind mine. Then he looked back to me, still smiling as he drummed his fingers on the door, and said without saying; *Lady, please get out of the car.*

I glanced around at the mess Josie and I had made during the two-hour drive then decided it could wait. I climbed out of the car, handed the attendant a five, and he got behind the wheel. He looked around the inside of the vehicle then back at me with a grin.

"What did you guys do?" he said. "Rob a candy store on the way?"

"Is being a comedian part of your job description?" I said, making a face at him.

"No," he said, laughing. "Consider it a bonus."

I arched my back to stretch and glanced at the rear of the vehicle where Josie was supervising the unloading of our luggage. When she was satisfied we had everything, she gave me two thumbs up, and I took a step back and waved as the attendant drove off. I followed Josie and another uniformed man who was pushing a wheeled cart containing our luggage into the lobby. We stepped inside and gazed around at the magnificent entrance. An antique stamped tin ceiling and a polished tile floor dominated the lobby, and it was accented with wood walls and strategically placed windows that put the finishing touch on the look they'd been going for. Chateau indeed. We took a few moments to take it all in then nodded approvingly and followed the wheeled cart to check-in.

"This place is gorgeous," Josie said as we passed a sign for the conference.

"It certainly is," I said, slowing down to read the sign. "Why don't we check in, swing by the conference registration area, then head up to the room? I'd like to grab a shower, and then we can figure out our game plan for the rest of the day. It's nice out, and there's a lot to see around here."

"Sounds good. But maybe we should order room service for lunch," she said, taking her place in the small line in front of the registration counter. "No sense walking the city on an empty stomach."

"Lunch? We just polished off a bag of the bite-sized," I said, coming to a stop next to her. "Not to mention the doughnuts."

"I need protein," she said, waving to someone she recognized. "There's Marjorie Steel."

I glanced in the direction of the woman who flashed a smile and waved back over her shoulder but continued hurrying down the hall.

"She runs that big shelter program in Toronto, right?"

"That's the one. Nice woman. She's one of the conference organizers. She sure looks stressed out about something," Josie said, then grimaced. "You gotta be kidding me."

"What is it?"

Josie nodded at the entrance, and I noticed a man chatting with a small group of people. He was holding one end of a leash that was attached to the collar of a Jack Russell terrier.

"Joshua Middleton," I said, shaking my head in disgust. "We should have known he'd be here."

"He's undoubtedly trying to sell more franchise rights to those monstrosities he likes to call pet stores," Josie said. "That Jack Russell is the official mascot. Middleton uses him on all the marketing materials and commercials. Cute dog."

"Unhappy dog," I said, watching as the man headed across the lobby literally dragging the dog by the lead. The dog pulled back but couldn't get traction on the polished tile and ended up sliding along the floor. Undeterred by the dog's protest, the man kept walking. "This guy markets himself as an animal lover? Unbelievable. Has he always been a total jerk?"

"Ever since I've known him," Josie said, shaking her head at the scene. "In vet school, he was voted most likely to get bit three years in a row. Oh, good, he didn't see me."

We reached the front of the line and waited until a young woman behind the counter waved at us. We stepped forward, and I grabbed my wallet from my bag.

"Hi," the woman said, beaming at us. "Welcome to the Chateau Lavalier."

"Hi," I said, sliding my driver's license and a credit card toward her. "I'm Suzy Chandler. We have a reservation for two nights. And I requested an early check-in."

"Yes, I see that here," she said, tapping her keyboard. "And you're here for the conference."

"We are," Josie said, glancing up at the ceiling. "This place is beautiful. Is the stamped tin the original?"

"It is. And thank you," she said, pausing to glance around. "It's a very special place. Okay, you're all set. I've got you in a two-bedroom suite for two nights."

"A suite?" Josie said, frowning at me.

"I upgraded."

"Oh, no. Not the briar patch."

"Would you like to hear about a few of the hotel's amenities?" the woman said. "We have a long list of guest services."

"Sure, sure," I said, nodding as I glanced around.

"How's your room service?" Josie said, flipping through a brochure.

"It's great. 24 hours round the clock. All day, every day as we like to say."

"I've heard enough," Josie said, grinning.

"You have WIFI available in your room, but we also have a business center should you need it. You'll find a safe in your room, but we also have safe deposit boxes available down here if you prefer. If you have any questions about what to do when you're out and about the city, just check with the concierge desk. They'll be more than happy to help you. Oh, and our fitness center is open 24 hours a day."

"Good for the fitness center," I said.

Josie snorted.

"Okay, got it," the woman behind the counter said, laughing. "But you can get a massage in the spa area."

"That might work," I said, nodding.

"And, of course, Zultan's Lounge is a great place for cocktails. It also serves afternoon tea if that sort of thing floats your boat."

"It doesn't even leave the dock," I said, shaking my head. "Sorry."

"I understand," she said, leaning forward. "I'm not much of a fan either. It's way too formal for my tastes."

"And the sandwiches are always way too small," Josie said. "Winifred's is located in the hotel, right?"

"It is," the woman said. "It's a great restaurant."

"The chef is a friend of one of our good friends," I said, then glanced at Josie. "Chef Claire will kill us if we don't stop by and say hi to him."

"It's already on the list," Josie said. "Okay, let's go register and get that out of the way. Thanks so much."

"Enjoy your stay," the woman said, then glanced over at the line. "I can help you right over here, sir."

We headed down a long hallway and followed the conference signs until we reached a foyer with several tables in a row organized by sections of the alphabet.

"Hi," I said to the woman sitting at the section marked A-D. "Suzy Chandler. And this is Josie Court."

"Of course," she said, smiling up at us. "You're doing tomorrow's lunchtime keynote address."

"We are," I said. "How many people have registered?"

"A little over 600. We're very happy with the number. Here are your conference badges. And some drink tickets for tonight's reception."

"Thanks. 600 is a great turnout. That's a lot of animal lovers," Josie said, nodding as she glanced around. Then she smiled and waved at the woman who was striding toward us. "Hey, Marjorie. It's so good to see you."

They hugged, then Josie glanced at me.

"I don't believe you know my business partner, Suzy Chandler."

"Only by reputation. It's so nice to finally meet you," Marjorie said, shaking my hand. "Thanks so much for coming. And I hate to do this, but I need to ask you a huge favor."

"Sure," Josie said. "What do you need?"

"I just got a call from Shirley Banford. She was scheduled to do a panel this afternoon, but she had to cancel at the last minute Would it be possible for the two of you to take her place?"

I glanced at Josie and frowned. Josie gave me a blank stare then spoke to Marjorie.

"This afternoon. Geez, Marjorie, that doesn't give us much time to prepare," Josie said. "What's the panel topic?"

"It's called Cash versus Care: Maintaining the Delicate Balance Between Economic Realities and Compassionate Service in a Rapidly Changing Marketplace."

"Catchy title," Josie deadpanned.

"Yes, it is a mouthful, isn't it?" Marjorie said, laughing.

"And you want us to argue the side of compassionate care," Josie said.

"I do," she said. "Now that I think about it, I don't know why I just didn't ask you two in the first place. But since you were already doing the keynote, I imagine I didn't want to burden you."

It sounded like Marjorie was talking to herself, and it was obvious she was definitely feeling the stress.

"I guess we can handle that," Josie said, glancing at me.

"Sure, we can talk for hours about that," I said.

"Oh, thank you so much," Marjorie said, relieved. "You're lifesavers. The panel starts at two, but you'll need to be there a few minutes early so we can go over the structure and do a soundcheck."

"Who's arguing the economic side?" Josie said.

"None other than our favorite money-grubber. Joshua Middleton."

"You mean we get to smack Joshua around in public?" Josie said, grinning at me.

"You do," Marjorie said, laughing. "But try and go easy. He's underwriting part of the conference."

"I'll pretend you didn't say that," Josie said with a frown.

"What are you gonna do, huh?" Marjorie said. "These things are expensive to put on."

"Sure, and you have to balance the economic realities of a rapidly changing marketplace, right?" Josie deadpanned.

"It's nice to see you haven't lost your touch," Marjorie said, going in for another quick hug. "Thanks again. I really appreciate it. I need to run. Nice meeting you, Suzy. I'll see you at the panel. And don't forget tonight's reception."

We waved goodbye then headed for the elevators.

"There goes our relaxing afternoon, huh?" Josie said, punching the button for our floor.

"It's only an hour and a half," I said, leaning against the side of the elevator as it rose. "I didn't know you spent three years with Middleton in vet school."

"I've spent years trying to forget it," she said.

"Am I picking up some history between you two?" I said, giving her a coy smile.

"He wishes," Josie said, stepping out of the elevator. "But he certainly was persistent."

"I see," I said, following her down the hallway.

"No, you don't see anything," she said, glancing over her shoulder. "Because there was never anything to see."

"Of course not."

"Knock it off."

"Somebody's grumpy. I think I touched a nerve," I said, laughing, then I flinched when she punched me hard on the arm. "Ow. That hurt."

"That's how you touch a nerve," she said as she opened the door to the suite. "But thanks, I needed that."

We stepped inside the suite and looked around. Our luggage was already neatly stacked along one wall, and the scent of fresh flowers filled the room. A bottle of champagne was chilling in an ice bucket, and an elaborate fruit and cheese platter sat next to it. I kicked off my shoes and glanced out the window at the magnificence of Ottawa, one of my favorite cities. The hotel, a structure that would have been right at home in medieval Europe, was perched on the banks of the Ottawa River and offered a great view of the Rideau Canal and the Parliament buildings. The fall foliage was on full display, and I felt a tinge of regret that we had agreed to do the panel. I would have much preferred to be outside enjoying what was, for mid-October, a gorgeous day.

"Good call on the upgrade," Josie said, sampling the cheese plate.

"Yeah. And check out the view."

"I'll be there in a minute," she said, eyeing her next selection.

Chapter 2

At a quarter to two, we entered a large meeting room and headed for the table that was set on risers at the far end. Two technicians were already waiting for us, and we tossed our bags on the table then stood quietly while the techs attached wireless microphones to the lapels of our blazers.

"Just say a few words, please. We need to check the levels," one of the techs said.

"A few words," Josie deadpanned.

"Geez, that's a good one," the tech said, shaking his head. "Never heard that one before."

"Maybe you'd prefer a joke?" she said, fiddling with her microphone.

"Sure. I could use a good laugh. And please stop playing with that," the tech said, glancing at the other tech who was now off to one side of the room behind the soundboard.

"What does a Dalmatian say when it's scratching an itch?"

"Oooh, now that hits the spot," the tech said, listening carefully.

"Oh, you've heard that one," Josie said.

"Yeah. But keep talking," the tech said, shaking his head. "We're still getting that hum, Jill."

"Where does a Rottweiler sit at the vet's office?"

"Anywhere it wants to," the tech said, then held out his hands and shook his head again. "That's a bit better, but I still hear it ." He glanced at Josie who was deep in thought. "You giving up already?"

"I'm no quitter," she said, laughing. "How about this one? What do you get when you cross a Rottweiler with a mountain lion?"

"No mail for a month," the tech said, then nodded. "That's perfect, Jill." Then he looked at Josie. "My mother runs an animal shelter, so I doubt if there's a dog joke I haven't heard."

"Cheater," Josie said. "Hey, are you Marjorie's son?"

"I am. I'm Thomas."

"I'm Josie. This is Suzy."

"Nice to meet you," he said, then frowned.

"Do you work here at the hotel?" Josie said.

"No, I'm just helping my mom out," he said. "What the heck is that? Jill, the hum has stopped, but now I'm picking up some sort of crinkling sound."

He glanced around just as I popped a bite-sized Snickers into my mouth. Embarrassed, I slipped the empty wrapper into my pocket.

"Sorry," I mumbled through a mouthful of chocolate.

A man entered through the double doors and paused for effect in the doorway. Then he strolled toward us staring at Josie the entire time. He was wearing an expensive tailored suit and holding a leash with the Jack Russell attached to it. The dog grudgingly did his best to keep up, but his head jerked every time the lead tightened. Josie and I flinched each time it happened, and by the time Joshua Middleton reached the table, we were both steaming.

"Josie! Well, just look at you," Middleton said, leaning down to slip the leash under his foot then moving in for a hug that Josie wasn't fast enough to duck. "Whoa. You feel good."

"Hello, Joshua," Josie said flatly, then knelt down to pet the Jack Russell.

"Please, don't do that," Middleton snapped. "He's working."

"On what, a neck injury?" Josie said, glaring up at him.

"You'll never change, will you?" Then he turned and gave me the once over. "I'm Joshua Middleton."

"Suzy Chandler," I said, reluctantly extending my hand.

As expected, he held it way too long and gave me a look that made me want to take another shower.

"So, I'll be debating both of you?" he said, glancing back and forth at us. "That hardly seems fair. But I'll just sit in the middle, and be *surrounded by beauty*. I do hope my fiancée doesn't get jealous."

"You're getting married?" Josie said.

"Yes, I'm finally ready," he said, nodding. "After playing the field all those years, I started asking myself, why do men keep chasing women they have no intention of marrying?"

"Probably for the same reason dogs chase cars they have no intention of driving," Josie said.

Thomas laughed as he slid Middleton's microphone into place. "Now, that was a good one."

"Thanks," Josie said, ignoring Middleton's instructions and stroking the Jack Russell's head. "What's his name?"

"Jack," Middleton said. "What else would I call him?"

"Russell?" she said, shrugging. "Who's the good boy? Yes, he's a good boy, aren't you?" The dog rolled over on its back as Josie began scratching his stomach.

"I really wish you wouldn't do that," Middleton said. "Jack! Sit!"

The dog sat on its haunches and hung its head.

"That's better," Middleton said. "Okay, let's get this thing going."

Marjorie entered, stopped halfway down the center aisle to have a quick word with her son, then continued toward us.

"Okay," she said, obviously still stressed by the sheer number of details she was trying to juggle. "Thanks again for doing this." She approached the table that was draped with white tablecloths and looked around. "Thomas, we're going to need some bottled water. And I don't see pens or notepads. Could you grab one of the staff?"

"You got it, Mom."

"Thanks," she said, nodding with pride as he headed off. "I thought we would keep this pretty informal. Why don't each of you open with a five-minute overview, then we'll just take questions."

"That's fine," Middleton said. "Do they each get five minutes?"

"I guess," Marjorie said, shrugging.

"Then I'd like ten minutes," he said. "In the interest of equal time and all that."

"Take all the time you need, Joshua," Josie said, shaking her head. "I'm sure we'll all be mesmerized."

"This is going to be so much fun," Marjorie said, grinning at Josie. "Okay, we've got quite a crowd waiting to get in." She turned to her son who was standing by the entrance. "We're ready, Thomas."

He opened the doors, people streamed in, and soon the seats were pretty much filled. I sat down on Middleton's left, about four feet away from him. Josie did the same on the other side. Middleton slid the end of the leash under one of his chair legs and snapped his fingers. The dog stretched out on the floor and inched toward Josie as far as the lead allowed.

"I'd like to thank everyone for coming," Marjorie said, addressing the crowd of about two hundred. "I'm sure you've all seen the title of this panel, but rather than try to recite that mouthful from memory, let's just call it: Cash versus Care. Basically, we're trying to get some insights about the best ways to provide great animal care and not lose our shirts in the process."

The crowd chuckled and gave her a golf clap.

"Representing the economic side of the debate is Joshua Middleton." Marjorie paused and waited out the round of applause. "As you all know, Joshua is the CEO of Middleton Enterprises, the largest pet store franchise in the U.S."

"And Canada," Middleton interjected.

"And Canada," Marjorie said, sighing. "How could I forget that?"

Josie and I glanced down the table at each other and grinned.

"Excuse me for interrupting, Marjorie," Middleton said. "But if anyone in the audience is interested in exploring the exciting possibility of owning one of our franchises, we have several staff members in the vendor exhibit hall who'd be happy to discuss it with you. And I will personally be in the exhibit hall later today from five to six signing copies of my new book; *Tales From the Cages.*"

By the time he finished talking, Middleton was puffed up and so full of himself it looked like he might explode. He glanced around the room.

"Does anyone have any questions for me before we get started?"

"Where's Jack?" someone in the audience called out.

Middleton started to frown but turned it into a smile. He reached under the table, grabbed the dog and held it up in front of him. The audience oohed and ahhed, then gave the dog a

16

round of applause. Middleton slowly lowered the dog below the table then tossed him on the floor like he would his work bag. Then he beamed at the audience.

"Jack's a bit tired at the moment. He's had a busy morning. But you'll see him around later."

"Okay, moving on," Marjorie said. "Discussing the issue of compassionate animal care are Josie Court and Suzy Chandler, co-owners of the Thousand Islands Doggy Inn in Clay Bay. And speaking from first-hand knowledge, I have to say that they are doing some wonderful things."

The audience applauded, and we gave them a quick wave.

"All three panelists will make some brief opening remarks, and then we'll take questions for the remainder of the session. Just raise your hand, and someone will bring you a microphone so we can make sure everyone hears your question. Joshua, the floor is yours."

"Thanks, Marjorie," Middleton said, getting to his feet. "If you don't mind, I thought I'd stand while I delivered my opening remarks. I like to move around."

"Good idea," Josie said. "I'm sure the snipers will appreciate the challenge." Then she flushed beet red and glanced down at her microphone. "Oh, is this thing on?"

"Smooth," I said, laughing.

As Middleton started pacing back and forth in front of the table, I glanced around at the audience. I recognized a couple of people, but it was mostly a sea of faces. That is, it was until my eyes landed on a woman sitting in the front row staring intensely at Middleton. Stunned, I glanced down the table to catch Josie's eye. But she was staring out at the audience.

I flipped the switch on my microphone to off and leaned toward her.

"Pssst," I said, loud enough to get her attention. She glanced at me, and I nodded my head at the front row. "Check out the blonde in the front row."

Josie glanced around, then shook her head, confused about who I was referring to. I nodded at the front row and surreptitiously pointed at the woman. Then Josie's mouth dropped, and she sat back in her chair. Then the woman took her eyes off Middleton long enough to grin and give us a small wave. We waved back, then Josie lost interest and reached under the table. I glanced over and saw the Jack Russell, off its lead and sitting on her lap, munching on the dog treats Josie was feeding to him one at a time. Middleton continued droning on about the rapid recovery of franchise fees through the use of judicious buying practices, oblivious to what was going on behind him.

Josie placed the Jack Russell on the table and reached into her bag. She removed a tennis ball and glanced down the table at me. I smiled and nodded, then reached into my bag for the dog treats I always carried with me. The crowd began buzzing at the sight of the dog standing on the table. Middleton was convinced he had the audience in the palm of his hand and began walking back and forth in front of the table even faster as his voice took on the urgency of a Sunday preacher.

Josie rolled the tennis ball down the table, and I stopped it with my hand and left it sitting in front of me. The Jack Russell trotted down the table and picked the ball up in its mouth. I held out a dog treat, and the terrier gently set the ball down, ate the treat, then picked the ball up and trotted down the table back to Josie. A low chuckle rumbled through the audience. We repeated the process three more times until the audience was roaring with laughter.

"I know I'm not that funny," Middleton said, confused. Then he turned around and glared at us. "This is an excellent example of what I'm talking about when I say that animal care has its limits." He sat back down in his chair and watched the Jack Russell trot by on his way across the table. "Dogs, all animals, need to understand their boundaries. Jack. Sit. Jack!"

Jack was enjoying his snack and having way too much fun to pay attention to Middleton's commands. I gave him another treat, then laughed when he picked up the tennis ball, paused to scratch one of his ears with the ball lodged in his mouth, then headed toward Josie. The crowd continued to roar with laughter, and Middleton's scowl deepened. As the dog trotted past, Middleton reached out in anger and grabbed the dog's tail.

Either the dog had had enough of his owner, or he just didn't like having his tailed pulled. Or it could have been a lot of both. Jack dropped the tennis ball, then turned and sunk his teeth into Middleton's wrist and hand and held on for dear life. Middleton screamed in pain and grabbed his hand. The dog accepted one final treat from Josie, climbed down off the table onto her lap, then hopped down onto the floor. He stretched out on the other side of Josie's chair, his work apparently done. Josie reached down to pet the dog, then turned to look at Middleton.

"Good boy," I whispered.

"Let's have a look," Josie said, inching her chair closer.

Middleton reluctantly showed her his wound. She held his hand and wiped at the blood with a white napkin that quickly began turning red.

"He got you pretty good," she said. "You're going to need some stitches."

"I can't believe that son of a-"

"Microphone, Joshua," Josie said, raising an eyebrow.

"Right," Middleton said, turning his microphone off. "I can't believe he bit me."

"Rule number one," Josie said, laughing. "Don't pull his tail."

Marjorie approached the table and took a look at Middleton's hand and the bloody napkin. "Oh, my. We need to get you to a doctor."

"I don't need a doctor," Middleton snapped.

"I guess we're going to have to agree to disagree on that, Joshua," Marjorie said. "At a minimum, we're going to have to reschedule the panel." She turned around to address the crowd, then looked back at us. "Would you be willing to do this sometime tomorrow?"

All three of us nodded. Marjorie frowned for what must have been the hundredth time today.

"What are they supposed to do the rest of the day?" she said. "All the other afternoon sessions have already started."

"If it were me, I'd just open the bar early," I said, shrugging.

"What a great idea," she said, refocusing on the audience.

Soon the room was empty, and Middleton was on his second napkin. The blood continued to ooze from the wound, and his face was drained. The woman who'd be sitting in the front row approached and placed a hand on Middleton's shoulder.

"You poor baby. Are you all right?" she cooed, then smiled at me. "Hi, Suzy. How are you doing?"

"I'm good, Roxanne," I said, still amazed to see her here.

Roxanne glared at Josie. Josie returned the favor. Roxanne was a woman who could only be described as a world class gold-digger, and we had crossed paths with her a few times in the past. The source of their tension came from an encounter they'd had at C's one night when Roxanne was flirting heavily with Josie's boyfriend at the time and playing a little fast and loose with her hands. When Roxanne's hand roamed too close to Josie's dinner plate, she'd ended up getting stabbed in the palm by Josie's steak knife and ended up needing several stitches.

Josie maintains that it was an accident, and she's sticking to her story.

"Hello, Josie. Have you stabbed anybody lately?"

"Not yet, but the day is young," Josie said, returning Roxanne's glare. "You're the bride-to-be?"

"That's me," she said, beaming at Middleton.

"You all know each other?" Middleton said, thoroughly confused as he stared down at his wound.

"Yes, our paths have crossed," Roxanne said, then glanced back and forth at us. "Let's hope the third time's the charm, right?"

"Third time?" Middleton said, glancing up from his hand to stare at his fiancée.

"Long story," Roxanne said, shrugging.

"All the good ones are," I said, grinning at Josie.

"Did you bring your bag, Josie?" Middleton said.

"My vet bag?"

"Yeah."

"Sure. It's upstairs in the suite."

"You got a suite?" Middleton said, frowning.

"Yeah, it's great. Why do you want to know if I brought my bag?"

"Because I want you to stitch me up," he snapped.

"Are vets allowed to work on people?" Roxanne said, frowning.

"No," Josie said. "But since Joshua is such a dog, I think we can make an exception."

"Funny," Middleton said. "C'mon, let's go. Before I bleed to death. Roxanne, grab that stupid dog."

Chapter 3

Joshua stepped inside the suite and whistled softly as he looked around the spacious living room. Josie pointed to one of the bathrooms.

"Let's do this in there," she said. "We don't want you bleeding all over the carpet."

"I can't believe you have a suite," he said, following her into the bathroom. "The front desk told me I was lucky to get a room with a king bed."

"C'mon," Josie said, grabbing her medical bag from one of her suitcases. "Let's get this over with."

Roxanne strolled around the room and seemed to forget she was still holding the leash.

"This is really nice," she said, glancing out the window at the view. "It's a beautiful city."

"It is," I said, taking the leash from her and bending down to remove it from the dog's collar. I sat down on one of the couches, and the Jack Russell cocked his head at me. I patted the couch, and the dog hopped up next to me and nestled his head in my lap.

"Jack's not allowed on the furniture at home," Roxanne said. "Josh says he needs to remember his place in the pack order. Whatever the heck that means."

"Well, Jack's not home at the moment," I said, rubbing the dog's head. "Are you, Jack? What a good boy." I glanced up at Roxanne who seemed even more confused than I was. "Why don't you sit down so we can chat?"

"Chat? You mean, so you can get a whole bunch of questions answered?" she said, raising a finger at me. "Don't think I've forgotten. You're quite the snoop when you want to be."

"Most days, I don't think it matters if I want to or not," I said, shrugging. "It's usually not an active choice."

"What?"

"Nothing," I said, spying the bottle of champagne that was still sitting in the ice bucket. "Now, there's an idea. Would you like a glass of champagne?"

"Absolutely," Roxanne said, sitting down on the couch directly across from mine.

I opened the champagne and poured four glasses. I handed one to Roxanne then headed for the bathroom. I opened the door and saw Josie kneeling down and trying to clean Middleton's wound.

"Hold still," she snapped. "You're such a baby." Then she looked up and saw me. "Champagne. You're a lifesaver."

"Oh, thank you," Middleton said, reaching for a glass with his good hand.

"Hold still," Josie said, then shook her head and stood up to take a long sip. "How can someone be so afraid of needles and the sight of blood and still call themselves a vet?"

"These days, I mostly *consult* on cases," Middleton said. "I haven't done surgery in years."

"Score one for the animals," Josie said, kneeling down to inspect the damage. "Okay, I'm going to hit you up with a couple of shots to numb the area. You're gonna feel a slight stick."

"No problem. Ow," Middleton said, flinching. "You call that a slight stick?"

"Sorry."

"I bet. How many stitches am I going to get?"

"Just as many as I can manage to fit in," she said, casually as she paused to take another sip of champagne.

"Is this going to hurt?"

"Oh, you can count on it."

"You haven't changed a bit, have you? Ow."

"Well, I don't think I'm as tolerant as I used to be," Josie said, stabbing Middleton's hand with another shot.

"Ow. Geez, what is wrong with you?"

"I'll leave you two alone," I said, shaking my head as I headed back into the living room and sat back down. I waited until Jack got himself comfortable then raised my glass in salute to Roxanne.

"I heard them bickering," Roxanne said. "They know each other?"

"Yeah, they were in vet school together," I said, stroking the dog's back. "She's always talking about the people she went to school with, but Josie never talks about Joshua."

"They were probably sleeping together, and it must have ended badly," Roxanne said, frowning.

"No, I seriously doubt that. She would have said something about it, even as a cautionary tale," I said, then caught the look Roxanne was giving me. "Sorry. No offense."

"He's really not that bad," Roxanne said, looking off into the distance. Then she caught my stare. "What?"

"I'm not sure if you were trying to convince me or yourself," I said, topping off both our glasses.

"You must be wondering how I ended up with Josh."

"The thought did cross my mind," I said, chuckling. "The last time I saw you was at the reading of the Winters' family will. And soon after that, I heard you and Brock were getting a divorce."

"I had to get away from him," she said, taking a big gulp of champagne. "That family...now, there's a cautionary tale."

"Can't argue with that," I said, draping one leg over the other. "Can I ask you something?"

"Sure."

"Do you actively seek out rich men, or do they just sort of fall into your lap?"

"Oh, I seek them out," she said, nodding. "I found Joshua online, and then things sort of took off from there. You know, the falling into each other's lap part."

"Yeah, I got it."

"I sense judgment," she said, peering over the top of her glass at me.

"Maybe a little," I said, shrugging. "But, hey, it's your life. Whatever works, right?"

"I guess. But this one's not working," she said, reaching for the champagne bottle. "Actually, I'm looking for a way out."

"You're not married yet," I said. "How hard can it be to get out of it? Just give him back that golf ball you're wearing and be done with it."

"And then what?" she said, staring at me as she fiddled with the huge engagement ring.

"I don't know. Maybe be by yourself for a while and try to figure out what you want to do with the rest of your life."

"Nah, I hate being alone," she said, taking another gulp of bubbly. "It's bound to get better at some point. But he's such a..."

"Narcissist?"

"Well, there is that," she said, nodding. "But I was thinking more along the lines of control freak."

"Yeah, I saw how he deals with Jack," I said, rubbing the dog's head. "Is he the same way with you?"

"Pretty much. Apart from the leash," she said, shrugging. "But give him time, right?"

"I don't know what to tell you, Roxanne. But if you aren't happy, I doubt tying the knot is going to help much."

"It's not," she said, shaking her head. "But I need the security. What on earth are they doing in there?"

"They won't be long. Josie's very good at what she does."

"Well, I know she's good with a knife," Roxanne said, staring down at the small scar on her hand.

"That was an accident," I said, lying through my teeth. "And you were hitting on her boyfriend."

"Yeah, I guess I was," she said, then brightened. "Say, is she still seeing Summerman?"

"Not really. They're kind of in a holding pattern at the moment."

"Interesting. Now there's somebody I'd like to get my hands on," Roxanne said. "Is he hanging around Clay Bay at the moment?"

"I haven't seen him, but I imagine he pops in from time to time," I said, casually.

"Well, the next time you see him, tell him I said hi."

The bathroom door opened, and Josie came into the living room shaking her head. She tossed her medical bag back into her suitcase and sat down next to me on the couch. Joshua entered examining the thick bandage wrapped around his hand and wrist.

"Seventeen stitches?" he said, sitting down next to Roxanne. "I could referee a dog fight and not end up needing seventeen stitches.

"Now that's a great idea. Let's test it out," Josie said.

"What's that dog doing on the couch?" Joshua snapped.

"Resting comfortably," I said.

"Unbelievable," he said, shaking his head. "Okay, Roxanne. We should go. I'd like to get some rest before my book signing."

"Sure, Josh," Roxanne said, getting to her feet.

"C'mon, Jack," Middleton snapped as he reached for the leash. "Jack! Get down from there. C'mon, let's go."

"Lighten up, Joshua," Josie snapped. "And don't yell at him. All he's doing is sitting on a couch."

"Say, why don't you leave Jack here for the rest of the afternoon?" I said, glancing at Josie who immediately calmed down and nodded her agreement. "You two look like you could use some alone time."

"That's fine with me," Middleton said, glaring at the dog. "Right about now, I'd be happy to sell him to you. The ungrateful little-"

"Josh," Roxanne said, her voice rising, then she softened. "Try to take it easy. Let's go back to the room and relax for a while."

"We'll bring Jack with us to the reception tonight," I said.

30

"Fine," Middleton said, then nodded at Roxanne. "Let's go."

They headed for the door but stopped when Josie called after them.

"Joshua?" Josie said.

"What?"

"You're welcome."

He frowned at her, then pulled the door open and ushered Roxanne out with a gentle shove in the back.

"What a *delightful* couple," Josie said, staring after them. Then she focused all her attention on the dog. "Your daddy is an idiot, isn't he?"

"Roxanne's already looking for a way out."

"Interesting. But she doesn't have the guts to do it, right?"

"Nothing gets past you," I said, laughing. "Seventeen stitches? That's a lot."

"Yeah, I needed all of them," she said, grinning.

"Really? To sew up a dog bite?"

"No, I only needed four for that. I used the others to finish the needlepoint."

"What did you do?" I said, staring at her.

"I just wrote him a little note. Sort of a reminder," she said, beaming at me as she reached down to scratch the dog's ears. "He'll see it when he changes the bandage."

"What's it say?" I said, raising an eyebrow.

"*Jerk*," she said, gently rolling the dog over onto its back. "You know, it's been a long time since I did any cursive writing."

"You have terrible handwriting."

"Yeah, but I made sure I took my time. I had a heck of a time getting the K right."

I laughed long and hard, then a question came to mind.

"Is he going to have a scar?"

"We can only hope."

Chapter 4

After making several stops to sample various appetizers the servers were carrying on trays, we finally made our way to the bar, turning enough heads in the process to make the hour and a half we'd spent getting ready worth the effort. I'd opted for slacks and a blouse, highlighted with a silk scarf my mother had given me for Christmas last year. Josie had decided on a backless black cocktail number that I'm sure was the cause for the vast majority of head turns and second looks. But we both felt and looked great and were eagerly anticipating a relaxing evening with nothing on our to-do list except have a good time.

I shifted the leash I was holding to my other hand and glanced around the crowded ballroom for signs of Joshua Middleton. My search came up empty, and I glanced down at the floor at Jack. He was surrounded by dozens of partygoers, many of whom were beginning to lose their focus. I bent down and picked him up, and he gently licked my hand as I nestled him in the crook of my arm.

"We don't want you getting stepped on, do we?"

"Good call. The natives are getting restless. These mushrooms are fantastic," Josie said, polishing off the last of her snack and wiping her hands on a napkin as she searched the room for servers. Then she rubbed Jack's head.

"It's like his spirit has been broken," she said. "The poor little guy."

"Yeah, he needs to get away from Middleton," I said, still searching the ballroom for him. "All work and no play, huh?"

"Yet another victim of the soulless corporate engine. Society is definitely in trouble when even our dogs start suffering from burnout."

I laughed and took a sip of my club soda. "There he is."

"Where? I don't see him," Josie said, trying to follow my eyes. "Oh, got him. What on earth is he doing?"

"It looks like he's arguing with a couple of guys," I said, then flinched when I saw one of the men Middleton was talking with throw a punch that landed hard. "Okay, it's official. It's an argument."

"Down goes Frazier," Josie said, doing her best Cosell imitation.

"Wow. Middleton's out. Good punch."

"Who do you think hit him? Another satisfied franchise owner?" Josie said, sliding a few steps away from the bar for a better look.

"That would be my guess. He looks familiar," I said, glancing over Josie's shoulder. "Middleton is famous for not living up to his promises. Or he could be sleeping with the guy's wife."

34

"Or both," Josie said, laughing. "Oh, there's Roxanne. How do you think she's gonna play it? The outraged litigant or concerned fiancée?"

We watched closely as Roxanne approached the commotion. She paused long enough to glance down at the dazed Middleton then resumed her casual stroll toward the bar.

"Well, what do you know? Disinterested observer," I said. "Interesting choice."

Roxanne spotted us and waved, grabbed two glasses of champagne from a long line the bartender had pre-poured, downed one in a single gulp, then set the empty glass down on the bar. She elbowed her way through the crowd until she was standing next to us.

"What's going on?" I said.

"What's going on?" Roxanne said, glaring at Middleton who was slowly getting to his feet. "He called it off this afternoon. That's what's going on."

"*He* broke off the engagement?" I said, surprised.

"Yes. And he even took the ring back," she said, glancing down at her left hand. "I was going to sell it and buy a condo."

"I probably would have gone with a small country," Josie whispered.

"What?"

"Nothing. Why did he call it off?"

"He said I wasn't worth the effort," Roxanne said, tearing up.

"That's cruel," I said. "But, hey, it's not all bad, right? You said this afternoon that you were looking for a way to get out."

"On my terms," Roxanne snapped. Then she downed half of her champagne.

"Who hit him?" Josie said, nodding in the general direction of Middleton who was on his feet, but wobbly.

"I'm not sure. I didn't see it happen. But it's probably one of his franchisees. One of them has been hassling Josh for weeks. His story is that he was never reimbursed for some construction costs that Josh promised to pay for."

"Well, if his franchise goes belly up, he has a promising career as a boxer. That was quite a punch," Josie said.

"It's too bad he didn't kill him," Roxanne said, glaring at her ex-fiancé.

The hairs on the back of my neck tingled when I realized she wasn't joking. Her eyes were dark beneath the red of her most recent crying jag, and she was clenching and unclenching her fists. Then she nodded to herself and began to walk away.

"Roxanne," I said.

"What?" she said, stopping and turning around.

"Where are you going?"

"To mingle. What else?"

Then she adjusted her dress that hung off her shoulders, checked her cleavage, and slowly worked her way through the crowd, her eyes scanning the room as if she were searching for prey.

"Well, you gotta admire her powers of recovery," Josie said, taking Jack from me and holding him in both arms. "Who's the good boy?"

"Why don't we grab a drink and have a seat?" I said.

"Good call. I'll find a table next to the route the appetizer trays are using," Josie said.

"Okay, Magellan, you do that," I said, shaking my head.

I grabbed two glasses of champagne and sat down next to her at the otherwise empty table. Josie set Jack on the chair next to her, and he was more than comfortable sitting there taking in the party. Middleton was now sitting at a table nearby holding a napkin stuffed with ice to his jaw. Marjorie and her son approached him, seemed to offer their condolences, then she jerked back, obviously surprised by what she'd just been told. Then her son leaned in close to Middleton who listened briefly, then shoved the young man away. Before the situation escalated any further, the others at the table intervened, and Marjorie and her son walked away from the table. Josie waved and caught her eye, and soon both of them were sitting at our table.

"What was that all about?" Josie said.

"He's threatening to sue," Marjorie said, shaking her head.

"Who's he planning to sue?" Josie said.

"Everyone. The guy who hit him. The hotel. Me."

"You?" I said.

"Yes. He says, as the conference organizer, I'm responsible for providing a safe environment for all the attendees."

"I wouldn't worry about it," Josie said.

"Joshua lives to sue people," Marjorie said. "And he's got a small army of lawyers he loves turning loose. I can't afford to deal with that."

"Don't worry, Mom. He's not going to sue you."

I glanced at the young man and couldn't miss the fire in his eyes as he glared at Middleton.

"I hope you're right, Thomas," Marjorie said, then got up from her chair. "Now what?"

I craned my neck and noticed Middleton, now standing, doing his best to mollify a woman who was haranguing him. The woman continued unabated, and several people within earshot stopped what they were doing to listen in.

"What's she saying?" Josie said, cocking her head toward the conversation.

"Shhh. I can't quite get it," I said, concentrating hard. "Okay…scum-sucking pig. I got that one…swore your undying love." I glanced at Josie. "I'm starting to pick up a theme…whoa."

"What did she say?"

"I can't repeat it," I said, shaking my head.

"He's making friends all over the place tonight, isn't he?" Josie said.

"I need to get over there," Marjorie said. "This is turning into a total disaster. Remind me never to organize one of these things again. I'll see you later."

Marjorie and her son approached Middleton's table and were soon engaged in the debate. We eventually lost interest and sat back in our chairs to play with Jack. Then Josie spotted a young woman carrying a fresh tray of appetizers and waved her over.

"What do you have there?" Josie said, scanning the contents of the tray.

"Stuffed mushrooms, potato puffs with an amazing salmon and scallion mix, and bacon-wrapped jalapeno poppers filled with cream cheese. And those are the chef's famous corn fritters. But if you don't like spicy food, you probably want to stay away from them. They pack quite a kick."

"Perfect," Josie said, sliding a chair back. "That tray looks heavy. Why don't you sit down and take a load off for a few minutes?"

The woman glanced around the room, then shrugged.

"Why not?" she said, sitting down. "It's going to be a while before things settle down." Then she nodded in Middleton's direction. "Does he even have a clue about how big a jerk he is?"

"Don't worry, he's about to be reminded of it on a regular basis," Josie said, grinning to herself as she selected a handful of items from the tray.

"What?"

"Nothing. These potato puffs are amazing," Josie said, sitting back to give me enough room to reach in front of her. "Try one of those."

"Salmon? Not a chance. But several of those fritters have my name on them," I said, glancing down at the dog who'd gone on point when he picked up his first whiff of bacon. "Sorry, Jack. There's nothing for you here."

"How do you like working at the hotel?" Josie said.

"I really don't work here," she said. "By the way, my name's Bobbie."

"I'm Josie. That's Suzy."

"Nice to meet you. I'm just picking up a few extra hours anywhere I can find them these days. And my brother got me this conference gig."

"Your brother?" Josie said, scarfing down a mushroom.

"He's the head chef here," Bobbie said. "I hate doing this sort of thing, but I'm in desperate need of money."

"Your brother is a friend of our other business partner," Josie said.

"Really? Who's that?" Bobbie said.

"Her name is Claire, but she goes by-"

"Chef Claire?" Bobbie said, her eyes lighting up.

"Yeah, do you know her?" Josie said, taking a bite of one of the poppers.

"Of course. She was the love of my brother's life. Actually, I think she still is, at least as far as he's concerned."

Josie and I stared at each other then focused on the young woman who continued to glance over at the turmoil surrounding Middleton's table.

"Details, please," I said, leaning forward in my chair.

"Yeah, we're gonna need a bit more," Josie said. "Do tell."

"They were in culinary school together in L.A. and lived together for a while. Then my brother decided he couldn't hack it out there and left, but she stayed behind to open…a restaurant? No, that wasn't it."

"It was a high-end food truck," I said.

"That was it," Bobbie said. "After things went south, they drifted apart."

"Did she ever mention him to you?" Josie said, glancing over at me.

"Other than saying she had an old friend who was the chef here, not a word," I said, shaking my head. "So, you two have met?"

"Sure. I used to visit my brother out there, and I saw her all the time," Bobbie said. "I love Chef Claire. How's she doing?"

"She's terrific. We have a restaurant in Clay Bay, and we're about to open another in the Caymans."

"That's great. Tell her I said hi," Bobbie said. "And make sure you stop by the kitchen when you have some time. My brother would love to meet you."

"Do you know if they've stayed in touch?" Josie said.

"Yeah, a bit, I think," she said, frowning. "But it seems to have that high-school reunion feel to it. You know what I mean?"

"Sure, sure," I said, staring off as I recited from experience. "The old…*it's been a long time, you're looking good, how have you been, nice catching up, see you later, don't let the door hit you.*" I looked across the table at her. "That sort of thing?"

Josie snorted.

"You're a real romantic, aren't you?" Bobbie said, laughing.

"I guess I'm more of a realist," I said, shrugging. "You mentioned money problems. Did something happen?"

"I sunk every nickel I had into a business that went belly up," she said, getting up as another ruckus broke out at Middleton's table. "What the heck is it now?"

A man was standing directly in front of Middleton poking his finger into his chest and screaming at him. A woman was tugging at the man's shirt trying to restrain him. But he shook her off then threw a punch that caught Middleton on the bridge of his nose. Blood began spurting all over the tablecloth. The woman dragged the man away from the table, and I watched as Middleton rocked back and forth in his chair. Then he fell forward, his head bouncing on the table. Several people huddled over him, then Middleton shooed them all away. He got to his feet holding a napkin pressed to his nose, then staggered off in the direction of the bathrooms. Bobbie picked up her tray, waited until Josie selected a few final items, then gave us a quick wave.

"It was nice meeting you," she said. "Make sure you stop by the kitchen and say hi to my brother."

"Will do," I said, returning her wave then focused on Middleton who was struggling to walk without falling.

"Not one of his better days," Josie said. "And in a room filled with animal lovers. I guess he can't go anywhere these days without getting the snot beat out of him."

"I think he just walked through the wrong door," I said, looking off into the distance. "I don't think that's where the bathrooms are."

"I think you're right. But his confusion is understandable," she said, laughing. "Who do you think that last guy who punched him is?"

"I'm gonna go with angry husband."

"Yeah, that would be my guess. Well, it serves him right. Chase enough cars, eventually you're going to get run over."

"Exactly. Geez, it's really loud in here," I said.

"It is. And all the alcohol these people are pounding back isn't helping."

"You know what I'm thinking?" I said, glancing around the room.

"That instead of hanging out down here with a bunch of drunks, we should head back up to the suite?"

"Yeah," I said, frowning. "We're getting old, aren't we?"

"I prefer the term *mature*."

"Then let's do the mature thing and get out of here," I said. "And we're bringing Jack with us."

"Well, we can't leave him here," she said, getting up. "Besides, Middleton has other things to worry about at the moment. When you think about it, we're actually doing him a favor."

Then we flinched when we heard a blood-curdling scream coming from the back of the room. We stared off into the far corner of the ballroom and saw a dazed Roxanne wandering in a small circle. Then she screamed again and dropped to her knees. I scooped Jack up in my arms, and we walked over, inching our way through the crowd that had formed a circle around her.

"Roxanne," I whispered as I knelt down next to her. "What is it?"

"In there," she said, pointing to her right.

I glanced at Josie. She shrugged, and we carefully made our way toward the door Roxanne had pointed at. I slowly pulled the door open and saw the lifeless body of Joshua Middleton on the floor. His eyes were wide open, and he was staring up at the elaborate stamped tin ceiling. He was still bleeding profusely from the nose but was now sporting a white beard that had been formed by the foam streaming out of his mouth.

"What is that stuff?" Josie said, staring down at the body.

"It must be some sort of poison," I said, handing the dog to her before kneeling. I looked closely without touching anything and sniffed the air. "It's definitely some sort of chemical."

"Is he dead?"

"He certainly seems to be."

44

"Geez, another one? You know, we might need to consider a career change," she said, shaking her head. "Something that involves fewer dead people."

Marjorie and her son worked their way through the crowd that had assembled near the door. She glanced down at the body then clutched her chest.

"Is he dead?" she whispered.

"Yeah," I said. "It'd be pretty hard to fake that."

"Oh, my," Marjorie said, shaking her head. "What is that stuff coming out of his mouth?"

"It looks like some sort of chemical product."

"It's Drano," Thomas said.

"The stuff you use to unclog drains?" I said as my Snoopmeter turned itself on.

"Yeah," he said.

I stared at him, an action he soon grew uncomfortable with.

"What?" he said, eventually.

"I'm just wondering how you would know that?" I said, my tone accusatory. I raised an eyebrow at him and maintained eye contact.

"Suzy, dial it down," Josie said.

"What is it?" Marjorie said, confused.

"She's wondering if I was the one who killed him," Thomas said, laughing.

"Oh, that's ridiculous," Marjorie snapped as she shot me a dirty look.

"No, I'm not," I said, completely on the defensive. "It's just that you sounded so sure what it is."

"I'm positive that's what it is," he said, casually.

"Are you an expert in plumbing?"

"What?" he said, frowning at me. "Of course not."

"Are you trained in criminal procedures?" I said.

"No."

"Psychic?"

"Well, I am pretty good at seeing annoying people heading my way."

"Funny," I said, fighting back a surge of adrenaline. "How do you know it's Drano?"

"Let's call it a hunch," he said, pointing at the empty can of drain cleaner lying on the floor next to the body.

"Oh," I said, flushing red with embarrassment. "Sure, sure."

"Smooth," Josie said, shaking her head.

"Shut it."

Chapter 5

Swathed in a luxurious bathrobe that was like wearing a thick-cotton-massage, I ran a comb through my wet hair and looked in the mirror. I tossed the comb next to the sink and shrugged.

"Close enough," I said, then headed for the living room.

Josie was already sitting on a couch in an identical robe with her feet up on the coffee table and Jack draped over her lap. She was flipping through the channels, landed on the local news, then set the remote down next to her.

"We need to get a couple of these robes," I said, sitting down next to her.

"Yeah, I know. It's like getting a hug from the Easter Bunny."

"You mean, if the Easter Bunny was five-feet-tall and made of cotton, right?"

"Exactly. Well, it hasn't made the news yet."

"It won't be long. I just saw it on my phone."

"Pet store magnate poisoned at animal conference?"

"That was pretty much the gist of it," I said, yawning. "Man, those cops sure took their time. It must be boring to keep asking the same questions over and over."

"Well, you should know. They're just being cautious. It's a big story," she said, draping an arm over Jack. "And horrible PR for the hotel. Not to mention the city."

"Yeah. And there's, what, over 600 possible suspects?" I said, shaking my head.

"What do you think happened?" she said, tucking her legs underneath her on the couch. The Jack Russell stirred and gave her the stink-eye. "Oh, I'm sorry, did I disturb you?" She laughed and waited for the dog to get comfortable.

"I suppose it could have been planned," I said, still trying to organize the multiple thoughts that had been bouncing around my head since we first saw Middleton's body. "But my guess is that somebody just happened to see him walk into that storage room and, you know, *seized the day*."

"Yeah, that's my guess, too," she said. "How many suspects do you have on your list?"

"What makes you think I have a list of suspects?"

She glanced over and raised an eyebrow at me. I shrugged and forced a small smile.

"Yeah, dumb question. So far, five. But it's still early."

"Five? Let's see…the two guys who punched him in the ballroom, the woman who was screaming at him…how am I doing?"

"You're three for three."

"You're not thinking about Roxanne for it, are you?"

"Yeah, she has to be on the list. You saw her reaction earlier. And then she made that comment about it being too bad that the guy who hit him hadn't killed him."

"Roxanne is a lot of things," Josie said, shaking her head. "But she's not a killer."

"Maybe not. But she's really mad about getting dumped."

"She was even angrier about Middleton taking back the ring."

"There you go," I said. "There goes the beachfront condo. All the more reason."

"Maybe…but I seriously doubt it. Who's the other one on your list?"

"Marjorie's son," I whispered.

"No way. Absolutely not," she said, glaring at me. "You need to take him *off* your list, Suzy."

"He had motive. And opportunity."

"I don't care if he was seen carrying a case of Drano. He didn't do it. Knowing what we know about Middleton, there were probably fifty people in that room who could have had a good reason to kill him. Why are you obsessing about that kid?"

"I don't know," I said, shaking my head. "I guess it was the way he immediately jumped in when he felt his mom was being threatened."

"She's his mother. What else do you expect a son to do when his mom is in trouble?"

"You're probably right," I said. "But I just can't shake the idea."

"Families stick together, Suzy. You should know that better than anyone."

"I do. And if anybody threatened my mom, I wouldn't hesitate to jump in."

"Jumping in is a lot different from killing somebody," she said, staring at me.

"I guess."

"You'd really kill somebody if you felt your mom was being threatened?"

"Are we talking specifically about Middleton or just your average Joe Schmo?" I deadpanned, then grinned.

Josie laughed.

"I give up. You win. But the kid didn't do it," she said, putting her feet back up on the coffee table. She began thinking out loud, something I try to avoid since it always seems to scare the crap out of people. "Roxanne, huh? That's interesting...I suppose it's possible. Nah, it's not Roxanne. It can't be her, right? No, there's no way it's Roxanne."

We both looked at the door when we heard the soft knock.

"Did you order room service?" I said, getting up off the couch and heading for the door.

"No, but I could eat," she said, reaching for the menu. "Are you hungry?"

"No," I said, laughing. "Cool your jets. It's just that it's three in the morning and a little late for somebody to be dropping by."

I glanced through the peephole and frowned.

"Who is it?"

"It's Roxanne."

I opened the door, and an exhausted Roxanne greeted me with a small smile. Her eyes were still red, and her hair looked like she'd been raking her fingers through it for the past few hours.

"Hey, Roxanne. We were just talking about you. Are you okay?" I said, taking a step back to give her room to enter.

"Hi. I'm sorry to stop by so late, but I didn't know where else to go," she said, tentatively stepping inside. "The thought of going back to my room freaks me out. Hi, Josie."

"Hey, Roxanne. Have you been talking with the police the whole time?" Josie said, sitting up on the couch.

"Yeah, they just finished with me," she said, plopping herself into a chair.

"And?" I said.

"Well, they haven't arrested me yet, so I guess that's something," she said, glancing around. "Do you have anything to drink?"

I got up, poured her a glass of wine, then watched as she downed half of it in one gulp. I topped off her glass then sat back down in my previous spot.

"That's good," she said, glancing at her glass. "All they would tell me is that I'm a *person of interest* and not to leave the city. And I'm supposed to keep them informed if I decide to change hotels. They kept asking the same questions over and over. Then they'd change cops and start over from the beginning. They did that three times."

"I guess since you were his fiancée and the one who found the body, you're an important witness," I said.

"They think I killed Josh," she said, baffled by the idea. "None of them came right out and said it, but I know that's what they're thinking."

"But you didn't, right?" I said, raising an eyebrow.

"No, I didn't kill him," she snapped. "What? Now you're going to start in on me?"

"I'm sorry, Roxanne," I said, backpedaling. "But Joshua called off your engagement today, and you were obviously very upset when we saw you earlier. It shouldn't surprise you that some people might be suspicious and have a lot of questions for you."

"Some people? Like you?" she said, staring at me. "And please don't lie to me, Suzy. I've seen you in action before, remember?"

I was taken aback by her direct approach. I thought about it, then decided to tell her the truth.

"To be honest, the thought did cross my mind, Roxanne," I said, eventually.

"But if it's any consolation, you're pretty far down the list," Josie deadpanned.

"What?"

"You're not helping."

"Disagree," Josie said, sliding a bit further down the couch as the dog stretched out to his maximum length. "Look at it this way, Roxanne. The only way to eliminate you as a suspect is by asking a lot of questions and analyzing all the facts."

"And?" Roxanne said.

"And what?" Josie said, confused.

"And where does that leave me right now as a possible suspect?"

"Don't ask me," Josie said, nodding in my direction. "She's the one with the list."

We all flinched when we heard another knock on the door. This one was louder and had a more formal tone to it. Either hotel management or the cops, I decided.

"Now what?" I said, getting up and heading toward the door. I opened it and found myself face to face with two of the cops we'd talked to a few hours ago. "Hello, officers. What can we do for you?"

"We have a few more questions," the male officer said, peering over my shoulder.

"How did you know Roxanne was here?" I said, taking a step back to let them in.

"Roxanne is here?" the female officer said, surprised by the news. "Interesting."

"Not really," I said.

"Actually, our questions are for Ms. Court," the man said.

"What do you want to talk with Josie about?"

"We just have a few follow-up questions," he said, waiting for his partner to enter first.

I closed the door and followed them into the living room. I couldn't help but notice the man's hand briefly come to rest on his partner's lower back as she slid past him. The woman paused just long enough to let him know that she appreciated it, then the hand fell away. The cops shared a quick smile, then went right back to business.

"This is nice," the woman said, glancing around. "I didn't know the hotel had three bedroom suites."

"This is a two bedroom," I said, casually. "I don't know if they have three...hey, what's your point?"

"Oh, nothing," she said, grinning at her male partner. "Just an observation about the possible sleeping arrangements."

"For the record, if it were any of your business, which it's not, Roxanne isn't staying in the suite."

"I'm not?" Roxanne said. "I was hoping I'd be able to crash on one of your couches. I can't go back to my room."

"That is interesting, Shirley," the male cop said, grinning. "The scorned fiancée ends up in the same hotel suite as the sworn enemy of her dead fiancé. At three in the morning, no less. All sorts of possibilities come to mind."

"Pervert," Josie whispered.

"What did you call me?" the male cop said.

"I think you heard me," Josie said, not backing down from the cop's glare. "You said that you have some questions for me."

"As a matter of fact, we do," the cop called Shirley said, sitting down in one of the chairs. "This is really comfortable." She glanced around the suite and nodded at her partner. "Very nice."

"Well, the next time you two get a chance, you should check it out," I said, deciding to poke the bear. "But I imagine you'll only need the one bedroom."

They both flinched and shot me a dirty look. The man eye's narrowed as he subconsciously rubbed the wedding ring on his finger.

"We just saw something very interesting downstairs that we'd like to talk to you about," Shirley said to Josie.

"Sure, go ahead," Josie said, stifling a yawn.

"When we removed the bandage from the victim's hand, we were quite surprised by what we saw," Shirley said.

"Oh, you saw it," Josie said, perking up and tucking her legs underneath her. "How did it look?"

"What?"

"I mean, was it legible?"

"The word *jerk* was stitched into his hand and wrist," Shirley said, staring at Josie like she was from another planet.

"I'm so glad you could read it. I had a heck of a time getting the K right."

"What?" Shirley said, glancing back and forth between her partner and Josie. "Bill, do you want to help me out here?"

"I guess I can try," Bill said, apparently as baffled as his partner. "First, we're going to need you to confirm that it was you who stitched Mr. Middleton up after he got bit by the dog."

"I thought I just did that," Josie said, frowning.

"Just making sure for the case file," Bill said. "I didn't know that vets could work on people."

"They can't," she said, shrugging. "You're here to arrest me for performing illegal needlepoint?"

"Why did you do that?" Shirley said, getting ready to jot down a note.

"Because he was about to start bleeding all over me."

"No, I mean why did you offer to stitch him up?" Bill said.

"I didn't."

"You didn't?" Shirley said.

"No. He asked me to do it."

"Because of your shared history, right?" Shirley said, her pen poised at the ready.

"No, I'm sure he asked me because he hated the thought of having to go to the emergency room. I agreed to do it because he was bleeding like a stuck pig and I just bought the suit I was wearing. You ever try to get blood stains out of a cotton-poly blend?"

"Actually, our uniforms are cotton-poly," Shirley said.

"Then you must know what I'm talking about," Josie said. "In your line of work, that's probably a daily concern, right?"

"It can be," Shirley said, putting her pen down. "But try soaking the stain overnight in a solution of water and hydrogen peroxide. It's easier on the colors than using a commercial bleach."

"Thanks for the tip," Josie said, nodding. "I'll give it a shot."

I shook my head and glanced at Bill who cleared his throat to get Shirley's attention.

"Uh, okay," Shirley said, embarrassed. "Now about your history with the victim."

"What about it?" Josie said.

"Is there anything you'd care to share about that?" Shirley said.

"Didn't we already cover that earlier?"

"We did. Briefly. But that was before we learned that you had decided to do some creative needlepoint on the guy's hand."

"That was just a joke," Josie said, waving it off. "You know, a little *gotcha* for an old college acquaintance. And I'm sure Middleton would already be laughing about it. I mean, if he hadn't gotten killed."

"A joke?" Bill said. "Like a joke between two old friends?"

"Old friends? Absolutely not. I hated the guy."

"Interesting," Bill said.

"Not really," Josie said, shaking her head. "Joshua was very easy to hate. No offense, Roxanne."

"None taken," Roxanne said, rapidly working her way through her second glass of wine.

"Refresh my memory," Shirley said, pen poised. "How long were you two together in veterinary school?"

"Three years."

"You were together three years?" Bill said.

"We were at the same school for three years," Josie said, casually. "And we obviously were in some of the same classes together. And we occasionally ended up at some of the same functions, or ran into each other socially from time to time."

"So, you're saying you knew him well?" Shirley said.

"Well enough to know that he was someone I wanted to avoid," Josie said, starting to lose patience with the repetitive line of questioning. "Why don't we cut to the chase? Just ask me what you want to know."

"Were you two ever an item?" Bill said.

"Never," Josie said as a simple statement of fact.

"Ever sleep with him?" Shirley said.

"Not a chance."

"Date?"

"Nope."

"Flirt?"

"He did, quite often."

"And?"

"I always found it to be a real appetite killer."

"Are you sure?"

"As sure as I am that you two are really starting to annoy me," she said, glancing at me. "Can you believe these two?"

"So, we've touched a nerve?" Bill said. "I think we touched a nerve, Shirley."

"I think you're right," she said, scribbling a note.

"Guys, as much as I'm enjoying listening to whatever brand of foreplay you two are currently using on each other, I'd really like to get some sleep," I said. "And I imagine the two of you wouldn't mind heading off and hitting the sack as well."

They both flinched at the foreplay comment and fell silent. Josie glanced back and forth at them with a big grin on her face.

"I think you touched a nerve," she said, glancing at me.

"That was uncalled for," Shirley said.

"We're just trying to do our job," Bill snapped.

"Well, I think it's time for you to do it somewhere else," Josie said.

"We'd like to get your fingerprints if you don't mind," Bill said.

"What?" Josie said.

"Did you recover some prints from the can of Drano?" I said as my Snoopmeter turned itself on.

"What business is that of yours?" Bill said.

"Probably none," I said, shrugging. "But why else would you want her prints?"

"For the case file, primarily. And we'll also want yours at some point," he said. "But, yes, we did get some prints."

"A man's prints, right?" I said, raising an eyebrow.

"How on earth did you know that?" Bill said.

"I've been sitting here thinking about it, and it's the only logical explanation," I said. "Middleton was a big guy. And whoever killed him had to be strong enough to hold him with one arm and then pour the drain cleaner down his throat. Josie's pretty tough, but she's not strong enough to do that. Not to mention that she was wearing a skintight cocktail dress and four-inch heels at the time."

"It wasn't that tight," Josie said, making a face at me.

"She could have knocked him out and then poured the drain cleaner down his throat while he was laying on the floor," Shirley said."

"But he didn't have a bump on his head," I said.

"No, he didn't," Bill said. "But he had been punched in the face twice earlier. He could have easily passed out on the floor."

"No, you're reaching too far," I said, shaking my head. "If the killer had found him like that, whoever it was would have had to kneel down to get close to the body. Middleton was still bleeding pretty heavily from the nose. You would have seen some smudges in the blood on the floor and maybe some footprints. From what I saw, there was nothing like that anywhere in sight."

"This coming from the woman who missed the can of Drano right next to the body," Josie said, laughing.

"Shut it. And if you check Josie's dress, you aren't going to find any blood. Which makes sense since she was sitting next to me the whole time. And we were at least a hundred feet from where it happened."

"She could have slipped away, taken care of Middleton, and then come back," Bill said, half-heartedly.

"C'mon, Bill. You can do better than that," I said, shaking my head again. "I'm pretty sure somebody came up from behind Middleton and surprised him, grabbed him around the neck with one hand, and then used the other to pour the drain cleaner down his throat."

"Maybe," he said. "But I'd still like to get a set of her prints."

"Or at least her phone number," Roxanne said, laughing.

"That's not funny," Shirley said, glaring at Roxanne.

"Sorry," Roxanne said, then glanced over at me. "Nerve touch."

I snorted then felt another wave of fatigue wash over me. I glanced at the clock that was approaching half-past three.

"We just have a couple more questions," Bill said.

"I think I can help you guys wrap things up," Josie said.

"Go ahead," Shirley said, sitting back in her chair.

61

"You both believe me when I tell you that I hated the guy for years, right?"

They glanced at each other and nodded, conceding the point.

"And when I tell you that he made my flesh crawl the first time I met him, you can buy that, too?"

"Yeah," Shirley said. "I can believe that. So?"

"So, if I had Middleton in my sights and was determined to kill him, he never would have made it out of vet school."

"Well played," I said, laughing.

"Thanks," Josie said, then focused on the two cops. "Are we done here?"

"Yeah, we're done," Bill said. "For now. But we're going to have to ask you not to leave the hotel until we get a bit further along in our investigation."

"Oh, no." Josie grabbed the remote with one hand, reached for the room service menu with the other, then stretched out with her feet on the coffee table. "Not the briar patch."

Chapter 6

"Getting ready for a long day of lumberjacking?" I said, staring in disbelief at the mound of food piled on Josie's plate.

"Shut it," she said, sitting down at a table near the breakfast buffet. "Besides, how am I supposed to know which ones I want to have seconds of if I don't try them all?"

"That sounds a lot like Roxanne's strategy with men," I said, laughing.

"Don't be disgusting," she said as she shoveled what looked like half a pancake into her mouth and dribbled syrup down her chin.

"Yeah, nobody wants that," I deadpanned. "She asked me if it was okay for her to sleep on the couch again tonight."

"She asked me, too. I'm fine with it. You?"

"Sure," I said, shrugging. "She seems pretty harmless."

"So, now you believe me that she didn't kill Middleton?" she said, turning her attention to a pile of home fries.

"Maybe," I said, frowning. "Yeah, I think we can take her off our list of suspects."

Josie paused just as the fork reached her mouth and frowned.

"Okay," I said, nodding. "My list, not ours."

"Thank you," she said, then put her fork back in gear.

"What are your plans for the morning?"

"I thought I might check out a couple of the workshops. There's one for vets on palliative care that looks interesting. What about you?"

"I'm going to try to track down the three people who had confrontations with Middleton last night before he got Drano-ed."

"Drano-ed?" she said, putting her fork down long enough to take a sip of water. "Your term, I assume?"

"Yeah. Not bad, huh?" I said, yawning. "Man, I'm tired. And I was hoping to take a walk at some point, but it's supposed to rain all day."

"You could always stop by the fitness center. I'm sure they have treadmills." She caught the look I was giving her, then went back to her dwindling stack of pancakes. "Sorry, I forgot who I was talking to for a moment."

"But on the way here this morning, we did *walk past* the fitness center," I said, nodding to myself. "I'm gonna count it."

"There you go," she said, laughing. "And don't forget that we need to stop by the kitchen later to say hi to the chef."

"That's right. Let's do it this afternoon after our presentation," I said, polishing off the last of my eggs. "And we need to track down somebody from Middleton's company about what their plans are for Jack."

"I'd like to take him home with us," Josie said, pushing her plate away. "I'm such a little piggy."

"Do you think we can get them to agree to that?"

"Agree to let us have the dog or the fact that I'm a piggy?"

I laughed. She wiped her mouth then stood and glanced around the room.

"I'll meet you back here around 11:30, and we'll go through our session one more time," she said.

"Sounds great," I said, getting up.

"You got your snoop-strategy all worked out?"

"Yeah, it's pretty much the usual. I'm gonna track them down one at a time and just start asking a bunch of questions."

"Ah, an oldie but a goodie," she said, nodding. "Okay, Snoopmeister. Go forth and annoy."

I checked the names of the three people I wanted to talk to, compared it with the conference schedule of events, and hit the motherlode right out of the gate. The woman who'd screamed at Middleton last night was one of the morning presenters, and I headed for the room where, if the short blurb about the session was to be believed, she'd be regaling the audience on the amazing market opportunities of animal massage therapy.

I found the room empty except for a woman at the front who was organizing her materials and testing the projection screen. She glanced up when she saw me, flashed a quick smile, then went back to what she was doing.

"Good morning," I said.

"Hi," she said, not looking up. "We'll be getting started in about twenty minutes."

"Are you, Wilma Firestone?"

She paused to look up at me and nod. "Yes, are you here for the session?"

"No, I can't stay," I said, glancing up at the photo on the screen of a Golden Retriever getting a massage.

"Are you a cop?" she said, finally giving me her full attention.

"No," I said, focusing on the photo. "Are those your hands in the picture?"

"Yes," she said, glancing up at it. "And that's my dog, Goldie."

"She seems to be enjoying her massage," I said, nodding. "Is that what you do for a living?"

"It's a sideline, but it's starting to take off," she said, brushing her hair back from her face. "I'm a full-time massage therapist. You know, on people."

"Sure, sure."

"You should book a session. Your dog will love it," she said, flipping through a binder.

"I think my dogs are spoiled enough already," I said, laughing.

"Dogs? As in plural?"

"Yup. The latest count is sixty-seven."

"You have sixty-seven dogs?" she said, baffled.

"Yeah. But the number fluctuates."

"If they were cats, people would probably want to lock you up," she said.

"No, I'm not one of those crazy cat ladies," I said, shaking my head. "They're okay, but I sort of got turned off to them when one of my ex-boyfriends compared me to a cat. We were out on a date, and it was sort of a mood killer. Now that I think about it, it didn't do much for the relationship as a whole."

She raised an eyebrow at me and waited.

"He said I reminded him of a cat because one minute he'd be hearing a contented purr, and the next I'd be off chasing a sock he'd left on the floor."

"That's funny," she said, chuckling.

"Yeah, he thought so, too," I said, shrugging. "At the time, I didn't find the humor in it."

"But it stuck with you, right?"

"Oh, does it show?" I deadpanned, then grinned at her.

"Okay, if you aren't here for the session, and you aren't a cop, how can I help you?" she said, sitting down and folding her hands in front of her.

"I just have a few questions I'd like to ask you," I said, sitting down next to her.

"I spent all last night answering questions," she said, staring at me. "Why should I answer any of yours?"

"I really can't give you a good reason," I said, shrugging.

"Excuse me for sounding rude, but you're coming across as a very strange woman," she said. "Who are you?"

"Yeah, I get that a lot," I said, nodding. "My name is Suzy Chandler."

She seemed to recognize the name and squinted as she tried to recall it.

"You're the one who runs the dog hotel in Clay Bay, right?"

"Well, we do a lot of other things besides the hotel, but, yes, that's me."

"I just read an article about you," she said, leaning back in her chair to give me the once-over. "It said that you always somehow manage to find yourself in the middle of murder cases."

"Yeah, I really need to start working on that. But it's sort of a hobby."

"The article said you have a gift for solving crimes. Some sort of sixth sense."

"That article cost me a small fortune."

She frowned, not sure if I was joking or not.

"Just kidding. The person who wrote that was merely being kind. Actually, if you want to know the truth, I'm just incredibly nosy."

"And now you're trying to figure out who killed Middleton?"

"Well, I had a little time to kill before our session later on," I said, shrugging. "But since you brought Middleton up, I couldn't help but overhear you screaming at him last night."

It wasn't the smoothest transition I'd ever come up with, but she seemed okay with it.

"A lot of people heard me," she said. "And most of them weren't shy about telling the police what I'd done."

"It was pretty hard to miss," I said, casually.

"And you think I might have killed him?" she said, giving me a hard stare.

"I have no idea. But I can certainly understand why someone might want to."

"Okay, I'll play," she said, smiling as she draped one leg over the other. "Based on what you heard last night, what was my motive?"

"I've been thinking about that a lot," I said, leaning forward. "At first, I thought it was just a relationship, or maybe an affair, that went bad."

"At first?"

"Yeah, but I think it's more complicated than that," I said.

"Is this the part where you're going to dazzle me with your brilliance?" she said, laughing.

"No, this is the part where I try to verbalize some of the goofy ideas running around my head and hope I don't come across as a total idiot."

"Did you watch a lot of Columbo growing up?"

"A ton. I still do," I said, nodding. "If you're comparing me to him, I'm going to take that as a compliment."

"It wasn't meant as a compliment. I was referring to the annoyance factor."

"Got it," I said. "Okay, here goes nothing. Since you started out as a massage therapist, I'm going to take a guess that Middleton used to be a client of yours. That's probably where you first met. How am I doing so far?"

"I'm still listening," she said, flatly.

"Good. I'm one for one," I said, nodding. "Then, over time, you and he started seeing each other outside of, let's call it, the clinical setting."

"You mean, I started sleeping with him, right?"

"Your words, not mine," I said, shrugging. "But yeah, that's what I'm saying."

"What if we did?"

"Nothing. You're both adults. And I'm sure Middleton might have had…certain qualities you found interesting. At least, in the beginning. And then you came up with a business idea that had the potential to change your life."

"Who have you been talking to?"

"Just myself," I said, shrugging. "Now that I know what you do, I'm going to guess that your business idea was to get into animal massage therapy in a big way." I paused to gauge her reaction. I got a mild flinch out of her and decided I was definitely on the right track. "And who better to help you do that than the guy who owned the largest pet store franchise in North America. After you outlined what you wanted to do, Middleton agreed to let you set up animal massage in all his franchises, didn't he?"

"Yes, he did," she said, baffled, yet still tearing up. "The Firestone AMCs."

She noticed the frown on my face and continued.

"Animal Massage Centers."

"Cool name. But then he reneged on the deal, didn't he?"

"Yeah. He cut me out of it, stole the idea, and was planning on doing it himself," she snapped.

"And you thought the perfect place to confront him about it would be here at this conference," I said, fiddling with a loose button on my blouse. Then I glanced over at her and found her staring back at me with a look of amazement.

"Actually, it was my lawyer's idea," she said softly. "He thought that if I could provoke Middleton into an argument, he might slip up and confess a few things we could use in the lawsuit. Not to mention the number of witnesses we'd have at our disposal."

"Good plan," I said, nodding. "But he hadn't started setting up these AMCs, and now that he's dead, it's unlikely the idea will get off the ground."

"We're going to keep an eye on what his company does, but I doubt it."

"And there goes your lawsuit," I said.

"Yeah. Along with my motive for killing him," she said, forcing a small smile. "I can't really sue a dead guy for something he was thinking about doing, can I?"

"Well, I know some lawyers who'd be willing to give it a shot, but, no, I seriously doubt it."

"So, the last thing I would want is Middleton dead," she said. "End of story."

Maybe, I thought to myself. I considered ending the conversation and walking away but decided to tread into a dangerous area.

"Were you still sleeping together?" I said, getting ready to flinch at her reaction. Fortunately, despite her anger, she remained calm.

"What?" she whispered.

"I'm sorry. But the other half of your potential motive is the relationship side. Some of your comments last night were obviously directly related to that. I don't think calling him, what was it, a scum-sucking pig was a reference to his business acumen."

She laughed.

"You should have heard what I called him right after that."

"I did. But I'm not comfortable using that kind of language."

"Too bad. It certainly got his attention. But to answer your question, no, we stopped sleeping together six months ago. Which was just fine with me."

"And that was right after you'd gotten him to agree to put the AMCs in his stores?" I said, again getting ready to duck.

Her face turned bright red, and she gave me a death-stare.

"That's a cheap shot."

"Maybe. Yeah, it probably was. At a minimum, it's a really tough question," I said. "I'm just looking for a motive."

"I think this conversation is over," she said, standing up and brushing the hair back from her face with an angry flip of her hand.

"Yeah, I was afraid you were going to say that," I said, getting up. "I'm sorry, Wilma. After last night, I imagine this was the last thing you wanted to deal with."

"Compared with this grilling, the cops were a piece of cake," she said, shaking her head. "So, Columbo, do you think I killed him?"

"I think you were probably mad enough to kill him, but, no, I don't think you did it."

"Why not?"

I glanced up at the slide of the Golden getting a massage and smiled at the look of sheer delight on the dog's face.

"I just can't picture the hands in that photo as the same ones that were around Middleton's throat."

"Thanks," she said, frowning. "I guess."

"And unless I missing something, I just don't think you're physically strong enough to have pulled it off," I said with a shrug.

73

"Too bad the cops don't feel the same way," she said, glancing up when she heard people coming into the room.

"I'm sure they're just casting a wide net and keeping their options open until they know more," I said, tossing my bag over my shoulder. "Look, I'm really sorry about all the questions. I know I can be incredibly annoying."

"Oh, so you see it, too. I thought it was just me," she said, eventually breaking into a small grin.

"Funny. Just try not to worry too much the cops. If you didn't do it, you shouldn't have anything to worry about. And, hopefully, when it all plays out, we'll have a happy ending."

"Now you sound just like Middleton."

"You lost me."

"Think about it."

I did.

Then I grimaced.

"Oh. Happy ending. Got it."

Chapter 7

Josie sat back down next to me and smiled and waved to the audience as the round of applause she was receiving continued. After doing a joint overview of our Doggy Inn philosophy and services to begin our luncheon keynote address, Josie had spent the last twenty minutes discussing the veterinary side of the business. While the crowd of close to six-hundred was obviously impressed by her expertise, they were blown away by our inventory of diagnostic and surgical equipment that, as my mother and the rest of the town council weren't shy about reminding us, rivaled that of our local hospital.

Now it was my turn to outline for the audience our rescue program that had recently been modified to increase the number of dogs we were able to find new homes for. I got up and stood behind the lectern, and glanced around the room where people were enjoying coffee and dessert. Just to my left, I noticed Wilma, the massage therapist, sitting at a table next to one of the men I'd been searching for since I'd finished my conversation with her. I recognized his face from the confrontation he'd had with Middleton the previous evening, but the thought that I'd seen him someplace else before nagged at me. My Snoopmeter immediately turned itself on, and it took me several seconds to get it under control. Nervous, but much less so than I'd been in the past doing similar presentations, I focused on my breathing, cleared my throat, and took a sip of water.

"Great job, Josie," I said, glancing over at her then back out at the audience. "And don't let her false modesty fool you. Without her skill set, dedication, and genuine love for dogs, the Doggy Inn wouldn't have ever gotten off the ground. She truly is an amazing and gifted individual. And I don't get the chance to say that to her in a public setting often enough."

Josie beamed at me, then got up and approached the lectern. She reached into her pocket and handed me a twenty-dollar bill. The audience chuckled. Josie sat back down, and I stared at the twenty, then at her.

"Hey, I said I'd do it for fifty."

I waited out the laughter then refocused.

"I'm going to spend a few minutes on our rescue program, a program we are very proud of. And I'd like to keep this informal, so please feel free to ask questions as they come to you." I gripped the lectern with both hands and glanced around the room. "Okay, I'm going to say this right up front. Those of you who are more interested in the profit side of the animal care business, are probably going to cringe when I share some of these numbers with you. To be perfectly honest, and incredibly blunt, from a money-making perspective, our rescue program is a total *loser*. It's what a corporate accountant with a science background might call a black hole in the profit universe. On a good month, our rescue program loses anywhere between five and ten thousand dollars. Each month it's like taking a handful of hundred dollar bills and tossing them into the wind. And you know what…apart from increasing the number of dogs we find homes for, we wouldn't change a thing."

I waited out an extended round of applause that caught me by surprise. I smiled and was about to continue when a hand went up. The man sitting next to Wilma had his hand in the air and a confused look on his face. Since he was someone I definitely wanted to talk to about Middleton's murder, I called on him right away.

"You have a question, sir?"

"I do," he said, waiting for a handheld microphone to be brought to his table. "Did I hear you correctly? Did you say that your dog rescue program loses around a hundred thousand dollars a year?"

"That sounds about right," I said, nodding as I glanced over at Josie. "Do you remember the final number from last year?"

"A hundred and eleven thousand," Josie said.

I glanced back at the man holding the microphone and shrugged.

"There you go, like I said, a black hole."

"That's insane," he said, shaking his head.

"But the recent expansion of our rescue program is going to allow us to test out a new business strategy."

"Which is?" he said, confused.

"We're going to try to make it up in volume," I deadpanned.

The audience roared, and I maintained eye contact with the man until the room settled down.

"Your partner mentioned earlier that you have a strict No-Kill policy," the man said.

"That's correct," I said. "We don't even like to *yell* at our dogs."

"But you must have a lot of dogs that people simply don't want," he said, obviously determined to make his point.

"We like to look at it a different way. We have several dogs that simply haven't found the right owner yet. And our job is to take care of them until they do."

"You never euthanize your dogs?" he said, having a hard time wrapping his head around the concept.

"Only when it's a medical necessity at the end of life to ease the dog's pain and suffering," Josie interjected.

"Absolutely," I said, nodding.

"While that is certainly an honorable approach, from a business perspective, it sounds, well, crazy," he said, nodding in agreement with himself.

A low rumble of anger and resentment started to build in the room. I held up my hand.

"No, it's okay," I said. "I started off by saying that some people in the room might have a problem with the numbers. But No-Kill, for us, is what someone who comes from a corporate environment, which I assume you do, would call a core value.

And as soon as Josie and I agreed on that idea when we first started talking about going into business, it established the framework on which we still operate."

"What's best for the dogs comes first," Josie said.

I nodded in agreement and waited for the man to comment. He seemed to be having trouble deciding which path to head down. If he hadn't been on my suspect list, I probably would have just moved on with my presentation. Eventually, he nodded and raised the microphone to his mouth.

"I could never run a successful business using that approach," he said.

"I'm not asking you to," I said, shrugging.

"Don't you have shareholders or a board of directors to answer to?"

"Well, we do have a small board of directors that meets quarterly. If you can call it that," I said, laughing. "It includes our other business partner. She's a world-class chef. And my mom and a few other close friends. But we usually spend most of the meeting eating and drinking."

"I'm sorry, but the thought of making the conscious business decision to lose a hundred thousand dollars a year doesn't make any sense to me," he said.

"Well, it's not really a conscious choice," I said, glancing over at Josie. "It just sort of happens."

Again, the audience chuckled.

"I can't believe any sane businessperson would choose to do something like that," he said, shaking his head.

"Yes, I can see that," I said, smiling at him. "But between the vet services and the hotel side, we generally more than cover any losses we incur on the rescue side."

"And if you don't make it up?"

"I write a check for the difference," I said, shrugging.

"You write a check. Out of your own pocket?"

"Yeah."

"Why on earth would you do that?"

"Because we love dogs," I said softly. "And I'm rich."

Another ripple of laughter filled the room. I paused to reflect on what I'd just said. It was the first time I'd ever publicly acknowledged that I had more money than I knew what to do with. I decided I'd said it as a simple statement of fact, devoid of boasting, and that it didn't bother me as much as I had feared it would for a very long time. Not that I planned on making a habit of it.

"And that's how you choose to spend your money?" he said, baffled.

I glanced at Josie with a frown on my face.

"Wasn't I being clear? I thought I made my point."

"Perfectly," she said, glaring at the man with the microphone.

"Thanks," I said, then I refocused on him. "Yes, that's how I choose to spend some of my money."

"Unbelievable. You call that a sustainable business model?"

"No, we call it a dog rescue program," I snapped, then my neurons fired, and I remembered where I'd seen him before. "But don't worry, we don't have any plans to sell the franchise rights."

He flinched, then glared at me.

"It's just that I can think of a lot better ways to spend a hundred thousand dollars."

I had to admire the guy's tenacity. But that still wasn't enough to overcome the loathing that was starting to work its way into my system.

"I'm sure you can. And I suppose I could use the money to buy a new boat or a Mercedes every year, but I'd rather spend it on feeding a bunch of hungry dogs."

I'd been so focused on the guy with the microphone that I'd forgotten there were six hundred people in the audience. As such, I was startled when they rose en masse and gave me a standing ovation. The man tossed the microphone on the table and glared at me. I waited out the applause, then focused on my breathing to calm down before continuing.

"Okay, I promised to talk a bit about our recent expansion of the rescue program. Josie and I haven't been satisfied with some aspects of our placement efforts. Our overall adoption percentage is pretty high, but we weren't happy with the length of time it was taking to place some of our dogs. The time from intake to placement is one of the metrics we keep a close eye on."

"Oh, so you do use some business metrics," the man interjected, apparently not used to losing an argument. "How refreshing."

"You're a tenacious little Greed Head, aren't you?" I said, raising an eyebrow at him. "Yes, we do use a lot of metrics. And while our rescue program may lose tons of money, I'm proud to say that we know exactly where every penny of it goes."

The audience roared with laughter, and, again, the man tossed the microphone on the table. He slumped down in his chair and folded his arms in front of him.

"After talking with our staff, we decided to take more of an active approach with our adoption program. As such, we recruited and trained a couple dozen volunteers to help us out. A lot of them are high school kids, others are local residents, many of whom are retired. After they complete the training, they select one dog and then use a variety of outreach strategies to find a good home for the dog they're sponsoring. It's been incredibly successful, and, to our surprise, about half of the initial adoptions resulted from the bond our volunteers and the dogs formed. After spending a few weeks with their dog, many of our volunteers couldn't bear to let them go. And since each volunteer can usually only adopt the one dog, we're continuing to add new volunteers on a constant basis."

I paused to take a sip of water and waited until the murmur in the room abated.

"Now, Josie and I are faced with a different problem," I said. "The program has taken off to the point where we don't have the time required to manage it. As such, if anybody here is interested, or knows somebody who might be, we're currently looking for a full-time manager to run our rescue and adoption program." I glanced down at my watch, realized that my time was running short, and glanced around the room. "Okay, let's take some questions."

Then I couldn't stop myself and looked at the man who was still pouting in his chair.

"I assume you don't have any more, right?"

I flinched when I caught the hand gesture he gave me that was hidden from the rest of the audience.

"That's not very nice," I said with a smile, then acknowledged a woman in the back of the room. "Yes, ma'am, what's your question?"

I spent the next fifteen minutes answering questions, many of which I redirected to Josie. We finished to a loud round of applause, and the noise in the room swelled as people made their way to the afternoon sessions. I sat down next to Josie.

"Great job," she said, patting my hand. "What a jerk, huh?"

"What else would you expect from Middleton's Chief Operating Officer?" I said, glancing over at the man who was in the middle of a conversation with Wilma, the animal massage expert.

"That's where I know him from," she said, relieved. "It was driving me nuts."

"Yeah, it finally came to me while we were going back and forth," I said. "I knew I'd seen him someplace before. Then I remembered he hit on me when we were at that conference in Boston a few years ago."

"Well, you handled him perfectly," she said, then leaned closer and whispered, "A COO punching his boss in front of six hundred people shines a whole new light on things."

"Maybe," I said. "And I definitely want to talk to him."

"You didn't get enough during your presentation?" she said, laughing. "Say, how did it go this morning?"

"It was interesting," I said, nodding at the table where the man and Wilma were still chatting. "That's her. Wilma Firestone. A massage therapist who's trying to transition into pet massage. She got cut out of a business deal she thought she'd made with Middleton."

"Interesting," Josie said, sneaking a peek at them. "Were she and Middleton an item?"

"They were. For a while anyway."

"But it didn't end well?"

"Oh, I'm sure it did early on. At least from his perspective," I said, sneaking another peek at the conversation.

"What?"

"Nothing. Not important. She's still furious about getting cut out of the deal."

"And now she's chatting with the COO. You think she's trying to salvage the deal?"

"Could be," I said, glancing over. "But I'm almost positive she didn't kill Middleton."

"Because you're sticking to your theory about how it happened, and she's just not strong enough to have pulled it off?"

"Nothing gets past you," I said, gently punching her on the shoulder.

"But he's certainly strong enough," she said.

"No doubt about it. You think the two of them might be working together?"

"You mean, they take Middleton out, he gets control of the company, and she gets her deal?"

"Yeah."

"Stranger things have happened," Josie said, getting up from her chair. "I need a nap."

"Me too. I don't function well on three hours of sleep. But we were going to stop by the kitchen and say hi to Chef Claire's ex."

"That's right. Yeah, let's go do that and then head up to the suite."

"Good plan," I said, tossing my bag over my shoulder.

"Great presentation."

We both turned to the voice and saw, Bobbie, the chef's sister, standing behind us.

"Thanks," I said.

"It was really good. And I loved the way you handled that guy," she said. "Hi, Josie."

"Hey, Bobbie. I almost didn't recognize you without your appetizers."

"That's because you never took your eyes off the tray," she said with a grin.

"Not funny," Josie said, making a face at her.

"Disagree," I said, laughing. "You're not working today?"

"No, I've got the day off. But I wanted to hear your presentation, so I just sort of snuck in."

"We were just going to say hi to your brother in the kitchen," Josie said.

"Cool. I'll walk with you. I'd like to talk with you about the job you mentioned."

"Sure. What about it? You know someone who might be interested?"

"Yeah, me," Bobbie said, nodding.

"Really?"

"Are you kidding? I'd kill for that job," she said.

"Oh, let's hope not," Josie said. "One a week is more than enough."

Chapter 8

Chef Charles, or Charlie as he insisted we call him, was a good-looking guy in his thirties with gorgeous blue eyes and an inviting smile. Apart from his looks, the other thing about him that got my immediate attention were the number of band-aids on his hands and fingers. I was used to seeing them on Chef Claire since she managed to cut or burn herself on a regular basis, but Charlie seemed to have turned it into an art form. It also appeared that he had a great head of hair, but that was hard to confirm because it was currently hidden under the large chef hat that he somehow managed to look good in. It was easy to understand why Chef Claire had found him attractive, and if he hadn't been the former boyfriend of one of my best friends, I would have been more than willing to let him know I might be interested in getting to know him a whole lot better. But since he and Chef Claire had a shared history, he was off the table.

He gave his sister a long hug, then shook hands with us and led us to the staff's break room off the back of the kitchen. We sat down and waited quietly until he returned with coffee and pastries. He served us, then sat down next to his sister and removed his hat.

For the record; two big thumbs up on the hair.

"How's Chef Claire doing?" he said softly.

"She's doing really well," Josie said.

"I'm glad to hear that," he said, nodding. Then he turned to Bobbie. "So, how was the presentation?"

"It was great," she said. "And you should have seen the way Suzy handled Middleton's COO. It was beautiful."

"Good for you," Charlie said, beaming at me. Then he turned back to his sister. "Oh, I think I've got another event lined up for you. Next Tuesday and Wednesday, six hours each night."

"Thanks, Charlie," Bobbie said. "I appreciate it. But if things work out the way I'm hoping, maybe I won't need the hours. Suzy and Josie are currently looking for someone to manage their rescue program. And the job sounds amazing."

Charlie frowned and stirred his coffee deep in thought.

"What's the matter?" Bobbie said.

"Do you really think that's a good idea?" he said, unable to shake the frown.

"What are you talking about? I think it's an amazing idea," she said.

"Working that close to Chef Claire?" he said. "It sounds…strange."

"You were the one that dated her," she said, laughing. "Not me."

"Yeah, but still," Charlie said. "I'd want to come and visit you. And I'm not sure how that would work."

"Oh, poor Charlie," she said, shaking her head. "You're unbelievable."

"What did I do now?" he said, glaring at her.

"I get excited about the possibility of finding a job that's perfect for me, a job I don't even have yet, and your first reaction is how it might impact you."

"That's not it," he said, fidgeting with his coffee cup. "It's just that you'd be so far away. And I like having you around."

"It's two hours, Charlie," Bonnie said, shaking her head. "Why do I even bother?"

"I'm just not sure if I can handle seeing her," he whispered.

"Then don't," she said. "I'm sure we can figure out a way for your paths not to cross."

"I wouldn't be able to be in the same town and not want to see her," he said, exhaling loudly.

I glanced at Josie who gave me a small shrug. Chef Claire had obviously gotten her hooks sunk deep into this guy, and he was still having a hard time getting them out.

"This is really none of my business," I said, glancing back and forth at Charlie and his sister.

"But that's never stopped you before," Josie whispered with a grin.

"Shut it," I said, then focused on Charlie. "It sounds like things didn't end well between you and Chef Claire."

"No, they didn't. But I'm sure she's told you all about it."

"Actually, no. She's never said a word to us about you. At least she didn't until she found out we were staying here at the hotel. That's when she told us a friend of hers was the head chef."

"A friend?" he said, crushed. "That was the word she used?"

I glanced at Josie who gave me another small shrug. I decided to be gentle but to play it straight with him.

"Yes, but she may have said, *good* friend."

"Typical," he said, slamming the table with the palm of his hand.

All three of us jumped back, startled. Charlie, red-faced, took a few deep breaths, then sheepishly looked around the table.

"I'm sorry," he whispered. "That was uncalled for. I guess I'm still having problems processing the fact that we're not together. Fresh wounds can take a long time to heal, right?"

"Sure, sure," I said, then frowned at Josie. "Fresh?"

"Yeah," Charlie said, holding his coffee with both hands as he took a sip.

"How long has it been?" Josie said, beating me to the question.

"Four years," he said, staring off into the distance.

Josie stared at me and silently mouthed: *Four years?* I rubbed my forehead and looked over at Bobbie. She had her head down but tried consoling her brother by placing a gentle

90

hand on his shoulder. He shook her hand away, then stood up and put his hat back on.

"If you'll excuse me," he said, tight-lipped and grimacing. "I have some things in the oven I need to check on. Suzy, Josie, it was very nice meeting you." Then he looked at his sister. "We'll talk some more about the job later."

Bobbie gave us a sheepish look, unsure of what to say next. We sat quietly as she formulated her thoughts.

"He can be very protective," she said, eventually. "And since our mom died, I'm the only family he has. He'll come around." Then she blushed. "I'm sorry. Here I am talking like I've already got the job."

"Don't worry about that," I said. "It's nice that he's so concerned about you."

"He's been…trying so hard," she said, tearing up.

I glanced at Josie. She seemed as surprised as I was to see Bobbie starting to cry. Embarrassed, she wiped her eyes with a tissue and exhaled loudly.

"Sorry. I still get emotional about my mom sometimes."

"There's no need to apologize," I said, patting her hand.

"What's the deal with all the cuts on his hands?" Josie said.

"Charlie's a total klutz," Bobbie said, managing a soft chuckle. "Always has been. I'm surprised he's still got all fingers. When he gets focused on his cooking, you better keep your distance."

"Chef Claire's the same way," Josie said, nodding. "She has this big yellow line in the restaurant kitchen she calls the Line of Death. Step across it without her permission, and you're liable to get whacked."

"Something you learned the hard way," I said, grinning at Josie.

"I still can't believe she hit me."

"You can't say she didn't warn you," I said, laughing as I remembered the look of disbelief on Josie's face after Chef Claire had smacked her hand with a wooden spoon she'd been using to stir a large pot of soup.

"Chefs can be so temperamental," Josie said.

"Well, that's Charlie," Bobbie said, nodding. "Look, I don't want to seem pushy, but I have copies of my resume out in the car. Would you mind taking a look at it? Given my experience, I think I've got what you're looking for."

"Sure," I said, glancing at Josie who nodded in agreement.

Bobbie got up and headed out. Josie and I focused on what was left of the pastries Charlie had provided. We both grabbed a chocolate cruller at the same time and silently decided to split it.

"Fresh wound?" Josie said, chewing slowly as she thought about it. "After four years?"

"Yeah, I know. Strange, huh?"

"I can't even remember the names of some of the guys I dated four years ago," Josie said, polishing off the rest of the cruller.

"But you haven't forgotten any of the serious boyfriends you've had."

"No," she said, shaking her head. "You never forget them."

"Still, four years is a long time to be carrying a torch."

"Unless he's planning on burning her house down," Josie said, reaching for a lemon bar.

"What?"

"The temper," she said, taking a bite. "Lemon bars have never been my favorite, but these are pretty good."

"He did sort of lose it for a second there, didn't he?" I said, eyeing the pastries. "Lots of bad memories buried somewhere."

"Buried right below the surface would be my guess. What do you think happened between him and Chef Claire?"

"Who knows? Maybe she'll tell us."

"If she wanted us to know, she would have told us by now," Josie said.

"Yeah, you're right," I said, deciding no on the lemon bar. "But I'm dying to know. Aren't you?"

"Of course, I am," she said, laughing. "But don't bug her about it or try to guilt her into telling us, okay?"

"Of course not. What do I look like, some sort of monster?"

"No, actually you look like a woman with chocolate in her hair," she said, pointing at my head.

"Really? How the heck did I manage to do that?" I said, examining a strand of hair.

Bobbie re-entered the break room and sat down, watching me closely as I picked chocolate out of a blond highlight.

"Did you decide to go darker for the winter?" Bobbie deadpanned.

Josie snorted.

"Funny," I said, deciding it would have to wait until I showered.

"I think she might fit in well," Josie said. "Is that it?"

"Yes," Bobbie said, sliding each of us a copy of her resume.

"Why don't you give us some time to take a look at it?" Josie said, getting up from her chair. "What do you think, Suzy? You feel like doing an interview tonight?"

"Sure," I said. "Why don't you stop by our suite at seven? That should give us plenty of time to take a look at it and get a nap in."

"Perfect. I'll see you at seven *sharp*," Bobbie said, obviously excited. "Thanks so much for the chance."

She waved and headed out. We collected our things and also headed for the door.

"You do know that we're going to have to run this by Chef Claire before we offer her the job, right?"

"I do," I said, nodding.

"And if Chef Claire isn't comfortable with the idea?"

"Then I imagine that Bobbie is going to be very disappointed," I said.

"Yeah, you read my mind."

"It's really not that hard to do."

"Then tell me what I'm thinking right now."

I squinted and faked deep thought then looked at her with raised eyebrows.

"The mouth on you."

Chapter 9

I showered, managed to get all the chocolate out of my hair, then slipped into my robe and stretched out in bed. But despite my fatigue, I couldn't get my brain to shut down. After twenty minutes of tossing and turning, I gave up and headed out to the living room. I sat down on one of the couches, and Jack took full advantage of my empty lap. Soon, he was softly snoring, and I was on the phone. I called the Inn first and explained to Jill there was a possibility we might need to stay an extra night. After hearing that everything was running smoothly, as it always did whenever we were away, I said goodbye to Jill and called Chief Abrams. He answered on the second ring.

"Hey, Snoopmeister. How's it going up there?"

"Hey, Chief. Our keynote today was a total home run. Yesterday was a bit of a different story. Did you hear what happened?"

"I doubt it. I took the day off and went fishing. My phone didn't ring all day, and I didn't even read the news or turn on the TV. Best day I've had in months."

"Glad to hear it," I said. "Joshua Middleton got murdered here last night."

"Joshua Middleton? The name sounds familiar."

"He was the CEO of the largest pet store franchise in the States and Canada."

"Yeah, okay. I got it. Murdered, huh? Where did it happen?"

"In the big ballroom downstairs right in the middle of a cocktail reception. Actually, he was killed in a supply room right off it. Several hundred people were there."

"Lots of potential witnesses," he said.

"Unfortunately, at the moment, it seems to be a lot of potential suspects," I said, stroking Jack's head who had woken up.

"Nobody saw it happen, huh? I hate when that happens."

"Yeah, me too. So, I was just sitting here thinking and thought I'd give you a call," I said, casually.

"I knew I smelled something burning."

"Funny."

"Let me guess, you've inserted yourself into the investigation," he said, laughing.

"Inserted is such a harsh term. But I do need you to do something for me."

"Suzy," he said, adopting the fatherly tone he occasionally used with me. "You need to be careful. I know you're in Canada and it's one of the friendliest places on the planet, but it's still a foreign country. And while I'm willing to give you more than enough rope to hang yourself, I doubt the cops up there are going to have much patience if you start snooping around and stepping on their toes."

"No, they're fine," I said. "I even let them fingerprint me."

"They fingerprinted you? What have you done, Suzy?"

"Relax, Chief. They fingerprinted everybody. They said it was for the case file."

"Okay, I guess that makes some sense. But that's gotta be one huge case file," he said. "They fingerprinted Josie?"

"Yeah."

"I would have loved to have seen that," he said, laughing. "How did she take it?"

"Not well. But at least she went down swinging."

"What do you need from me?"

"I was wondering if your buddy still works for the SEC?"

"Which one?"

"What?"

"Which one?"

"How many buddies do you have working there?"

"No, which SEC are you talking about?"

"There's more than one?"

"Yeah. There's the Securities and Exchange Commission, and the SEC, the athletic conference."

"Oh. I did not know that," I said, shrugging at Jack. "I'm talking about the one that's always trying to keep track of people who are trying to manipulate the system and doing goofy things with money."

"I'm going to need you to be a bit more specific," he said, chuckling.

"What?"

"I guess only a college football fan would get that joke," he said. "Too bad you're not. It was a good one."

"I'll take your word for it. Would you mind calling your buddy at the not-a-conference SEC?"

"I'll be happy to do that. Actually, he owes me a favor."

"That's great. What did you do for him?"

"I got him two tickets on the fifty-yard line for last year's Alabama-Auburn game. Actually, it was my buddy at the SEC who got him the tickets."

"Your buddy at the SEC got tickets for your buddy at the SEC?"

"Yeah."

"Somebody needs to think about changing their initials," I said. "Could you ask him if he's heard about any problems or turmoil at Middleton Enterprises? I'm pretty sure they're a public company."

"I can do that," he said. "And you'd like it as soon as possible, right?"

"You know me so well."

"What do you need it for?" Chief Abrams said.

"I kinda like the COO for the murder," I said, saying it out loud for the first time and deciding that it didn't sound too off the wall.

"And if there's some unrest inside the company, you think that might give you the motive?"

"Yeah. Does that sound crazy?"

"No, it doesn't. But killing somebody in front of several hundred people does. I'd expect a corporate executive to be smarter than that. And to exhibit a lot more self-control."

"Yeah, I keep looping around back to that. But if something really big was happening at the company, anything is possible, right?"

"Sure. Have you talked with this guy yet?"

"Well, I sort of got into it today with him during our Q&A."

"Of course, you did," he said, laughing. "What did he do?"

"He was bad-mouthing our rescue program. Said it was a total waste of money."

"Silly man."

"Yeah, we sort of humiliated him in public," I said, unable to stop myself from grinning at the memory.

"How did the audience react?"

"They gave us a standing ovation. Why?"

"Those guys don't like having the chrome knocked off their finish. Especially in public."

"Hey, he asked for it."

"I'm sure he did," he said, then slid back into his fatherly tone. "Just promise me you'll be careful when you do talk with him. If he was willing to kill his CEO, he wouldn't think twice about getting rid of you."

"Yeah, that thought has crossed my mind. But I've got the perfect excuse to talk to him."

"What's that?"

"We're going to take the company's dog off their hands," I said, scratching one of Jack's ears.

"Whatever," he whispered. "Just be careful, huh?"

"Will do."

"By the way, I ran into Chef Claire at the grocery store this afternoon."

"And?"

"And she was in a really foul mood."

"Chef Claire?"

"Yeah, you know, I think that's the first time I've ever seen her in a bad mood."

"Did she say why?"

"No. And I didn't ask. It was pretty clear she wasn't in the mood for questions, and, unlike you, I tend to give people their space at times like that."

"Yeah, I really need to start working on that," I said, focused on the possible source of Chef Claire's distress. "Let me know what your buddy has to say."

"Will do. When do you get back in town?"

"Hopefully, tomorrow. Unless the cops decide they want us to stick around, we'll probably get back late in the afternoon. Josie has her heart set on some Chinese lunch buffet she's been dying to try."

"That poor restaurant."

"Yeah, they won't know what hit them. And if I don't take her, she'll be complaining the whole ride home."

"Please, be careful," he said, again with the paternal tone.

"Don't worry, I always keep my distance when she's eating."

"You know what I'm talking about," he said, sternly.

"Will do," I said, laughing. Then I couldn't help myself from adding. "Dad."

"You should be so lucky."

Chapter 10

I tossed my phone on the coffee table and stretched out on the couch. Jack repositioned himself and was soon sound asleep. I closed my eyes and drifted off and didn't wake up until Josie came into the living room a half-hour later. She sat down on the couch across from me and made room when Jack hopped up next to her.

"Did you get some sleep?" I said, yawning.

"Yeah, I got an hour or so," she said. "It should be enough to get me through the rest of the day. Did you get a chance to take a look at Bobbie's resume?"

"I did. It looks good. I've got a couple questions about what happened to her business when she tried to expand, but other than that, I think she might be a great hire."

"She's definitely an animal lover. And she's done a whole bunch of volunteer work. You gotta like that. Did you call Chef Claire yet?"

"No, I was waiting for you," I said, reaching for my phone. "You want to do it now?"

"Yeah, we probably should. If she's not cool with the idea, there's really no reason to waste time doing the interview."

I nodded and placed the call. Chef Claire answered on the second ring.

"Hey," she said.

"Sorry to call you during dinner hours," I said.

"Not a problem. It's really slow tonight. And pretty much everybody who is here is having the special. I was actually thinking about turning things over to George and heading home. How's it going up there?"

"Not bad," I said. "Apart from the dead guy in the supply closet."

"What? Not another one," she said.

"Yeah, but that's not why we're calling."

"Oh, Josie's there. How are you doing, Josie?"

"Good. And you?"

"I've had better days," Chef Claire whispered.

"Did you get a phone call today?" I said. "A phone call that bothered you?"

"As a matter of fact, I did. How on earth did you know that?"

"We met Charlie today," I said.

"I see. And he told you he called me?"

"No, that was just a guess," I said.

"Well, it was a good one," she said, then paused for several seconds. "How does he look?"

I glanced at Josie who shrugged. I decided there was no reason to lie to her.

"He looks great," I said.

"He's gorgeous," Josie said.

"Yes, he is, isn't he?"

"Did he mention that we also met Bobbie?" I said.

"No, he didn't."

"Actually, she's the reason we're calling."

"Bobbie's great. If you see her again, tell her I said hi," Chef Claire said, then paused again before continuing. "Why would she be the reason you're calling?"

"Because she wants to apply for the Rescue Manager position," I said.

We waited out another very long silence. Finally, she continued.

"I see."

"What do you think about that?"

"Do you want my honest answer?"

"Of course," Josie said. "Why do you think we're calling to talk about it?"

"Thanks. I appreciate you doing that," Chef Claire said. "Then I have to say I think it's a bad idea. But not because of Bobbie. If it was just her, I wouldn't hesitate to say yes. Unfortunately, I'm worried about who else might decide to tag along."

"You don't think he'll be able to stay away?" Josie said.

"Charlie's never been able to do it before. In fact, I'm surprised he hasn't already decided to pop in. I guess the restraining order finally got his attention."

I stared at Josie, then decided to tread very carefully.

"Restraining order?" I whispered.

"Yeah. Long story."

"Maybe you can tell us all about it sometime," I said.

"Maybe," Chef Claire said. "Look, I'd hate to be the reason why Bobbie didn't get a job. Tell you what, if she can convince you that she can keep Charlie out of Clay Bay, I might be willing to give it a shot."

"Okay," Josie said. "And if she can't do that?"

"Then I'll be heading to the Caymans earlier than planned."

Chapter 11

Since I had an hour to kill before our interview with Bobbie, I decided to head downstairs to see if I could locate Victor Rollins, the COO of Middleton Enterprises. Josie begged off, citing the need for a bit more sleep, and I watched her head back to bed with Jack tucked under one arm, then got dressed and headed for the elevators. When I reached the lobby, I noticed dozens of conference attendees streaming out of their afternoon sessions, and since my initial encounter with Rollins had occurred around the same time of day and he'd been hammered, I decided that the closest bar might be the most likely place to find him.

My neurons must have been firing on all cylinders because I stepped inside the softly lit space and immediately saw him on the opposite side of the room standing with his back to the bar. He was scanning the bar like a ravenous shark that had stumbled upon a herd of seals at feeding time, and he kept nudging the man standing next to him every time he saw a woman who caught his eye. But when he saw me heading straight for him, he turned around and hunched over his drink, apparently in an effort to make himself look smaller.

Unfortunately for him, it didn't work.

I stopped directly behind him and cleared my throat. The man standing next to Rollins checked me out, gave me his best come-hither smile, and was about to speak when he caught the look on my face. He whispered into Rollins' ear, then grabbed his drink and made a hasty retreat. I cleared my throat again.

"Ms. Chandler, I presume," Rollins said, not turning around.

"Victor Rollins," I said, sliding into the space the man had vacated. "I was hoping to run into you."

"You want to take another couple of shots at me?" he said, glancing over at me with his elbows resting on the bar. "Or regale me with more tales of your remarkable ability to throw money away?"

"Oh, don't be like that Victor," I said, then ordered a glass of wine from the bartender. "And bring my friend another, please."

"Thanks," Rollins said, rattling the ice cubes in his drink then polishing it off. He pushed the empty glass away and stood tall as he finally deigned me worthy of eye contact. "What can I do for you, Ms. Chandler?"

"Please, call me Suzy," I said, taking a sip of wine. "I wanted to talk with you about Jack."

"Jack?" he said, frowning. "Jack who?"

"The Jack Russell terrier. You know, your company's mascot?"

"Oh, him," he said, frowning. "I have no idea what happened to him. If you want to use the dog in a promotion, you'll need to contact our marketing group."

"No, I don't want to use him for a promotion."

"That's good," he said, laughing then taking a slug of his fresh glass of scotch. "Because that dog is done. Or at least he will be soon."

"What do you mean, done?"

"Done as in no longer representing our company," Rollins said, rattling his ice cubes again. "The word is already out on the street that he bit Josh. And I'm sure at least a dozen people managed to capture the whole thing on their phones. We can't keep using that dog as our major brand representative after he tried to take our CEO's hand off."

"Middleton deserved everything he got," I snapped.

"I'm sure he did," Rollins said, nodding as an evil grin appeared on his face. "I'm just sorry I wasn't there to see it."

I frowned when a thought popped into my head. Rollins noticed.

"What is it?" he said.

"I'm just wondering why you're still here at the conference," I said, glancing over at him. "Your CEO was murdered here last night."

"Life goes on," he said, nonchalantly as he sipped his scotch. "And don't even get me started on the vampire-like qualities of Middleton Enterprises. That place will survive nuclear winter." He laughed, rattled his ice cubes, then gave me a boozy stare.

"And staying here to keep an eye on things is what Middleton would have expected?"

"No, it's what he would have demanded," he said, laughing. "Middleton's dead. And there's nothing I can do about it. Other than try to sell some new franchises."

"Nice business model," I said to my wine glass. "So, what are you going to do with him?"

"The dog? If I wasn't talking to you, I'd probably say we were going to put him down," he said, laughing.

"I'm going to pretend you didn't say that," I said, taking a tight-lipped sip of wine.

"I wonder where the heck the dog is," Rollins said, finishing his drink and snapping his fingers at the bartender. "You want another?"

"No, I'm good," I said, shaking my head. "And please don't do that."

"Do what?"

"Snap your fingers at the bartender like he's some sort of personal lackey."

"Isn't that what he is?" Rollins said, baffled. Then he cocked his head when he heard me mumble under my breath. "What did you say?"

"Nothing. But just so you know, I have the dog."

"What are you doing with it?"

"We were watching him for Middleton just before he got killed. And since Roxanne was in no condition to look after Jack, we've been keeping an eye on him."

"Roxanne," he said, laughing. "What a piece of work that little gold digger is. She was perfect for Josh."

"The perfect companion for a scum-sucking pig?" I said, raising an eyebrow at him over the top of my glass.

"That's right," he said, studying my face. "Wilma mentioned that you'd talked with her."

"How well do you know Wilma?"

"What do you mean, how well do I know her? What sort of question is that?"

"It's just a question. I noticed you were sitting next to her at lunch. And then afterward, the two of you seemed to be having a pretty intense conversation."

"What business is that of yours?"

Since we were in a crowded bar and I was pretty sure the last thing he would want today was another public confrontation with me, I decided to poke the bear a bit.

"Oh, I'm pretty sure it's none of my business," I said, beaming at him. "But I do find it interesting that the woman who had recently gotten cut out of her own deal with Middleton Enterprises, would be so *chummy* with the COO."

"What are you insinuating?" he said, again rattling the ice cubes in his empty glass.

"Let me get you another one of those," I said, giving the bartender a small wave. "I'm not suggesting anything. It just seems strange that Wilma would be so friendly given what happened to her."

"Wilma's problem was with Josh. We get along just fine."

"I'm glad to hear that," I said, taking a sip. "She seems very…agreeable."

Rollins flinched but said nothing. He stirred his fresh drink and stared down at the bar.

"Is her deal going to be resurrected?"

"Maybe," he said, nodding. "It's an interesting idea that could work in some of our markets, but a lot will depend on what happens over the next few days."

"You mean if the board decides to make you CEO?"

He grimaced and swiveled his head around his neck as if he was in severe pain. Or maybe it was just his way of showing annoyance with people who asked way too many questions.

"That's part of it," he whispered.

"And the other part is whether or not the police decide to charge you with his murder, right?"

He turned and stared at me in disbelief.

"Who have you been talking to?"

"Nobody," I said, shrugging. "It's just a hunch. After you attacked him the other night right before he turned up dead, the cops must have you pretty high up on the list of suspects."

"I didn't kill him. I was mad enough to kill him, but I didn't."

"What did he do that made you so angry?"

"That, most definitely, is none of your business," he snapped.

"Confidential business matters, right?"

"Exactly," he said, staring at me. "Tell me again why you're standing here bothering me with all these questions."

I wasn't sure how many drinks he'd had, but his speech had a hint of a slur, and his eyes were covered by a rheumy glaze.

"Jack."

"Oh, the dog, right," he said, then frowned. "What about him?"

"We'd like to keep him."

"You want the dog?"

"Yes."

"Why?"

"Because he's had all his spirit knocked out of him, and we think we can help him get it back."

For some reason, he found my comment funny, and he laughed long and hard. Then he wiped his eyes with the back of his hand.

"Tell you what, Ms. Chandler, if you can figure out a way to do that, make sure you let me in on your secret. Maybe we could work together and package it. We'd make millions."

Then he went off again. I ignored the condescending laugh and stared off into the distance until he finished. Then he rattled his ice cubes again. It was an annoying habit that was really starting to get on my nerves.

"It's really not that hard," I said, shrugging. "It just takes time and a lot of love and affection."

"Then you're definitely talking to the wrong guy," he said, grinning.

"You're telling me," I whispered into my glass, then glanced up at him. "Why's that?"

"You've never worked in a major corporation, have you?"

"No. And I can't think of anything worse."

"Well, there is unemployment, and that's certainly not a desirable alternative. You don't know what it's like to try to hit a quarterly number."

"No, I can't even imagine what it would be like to live my life in ninety-day windows."

"It's a relentless…daily…*grrrrind*," he said. "But I'm just trying to stay focused and keep my eyes on the prize."

"The workforce's getting nervous, management's acting squirrelly. You better hit it hard, and get out early."

"What? Where have I heard that?" Rollins said, frowning. "That's a song, right?"

"Yeah, a friend of mine wrote it," I said, singing the catchy chorus silently to myself.

"Hey, I know that song. You're a friend of Summerman Lawless?"

"I am."

"What's he up to these days?"

"Oh, I'm sure he's around somewhere," I said as I snuck a quick peek up at the ceiling. Then I gave him a small smile. "Your strategy is to retire early?"

"Yes. And hopefully on my own terms and timetable," he said, finally starting to relax a bit. "But if the cops keep me here much longer, I don't like my chances."

"They asked you to stick around?"

"Yeah, at least until they decide what they're going to do with me."

"Well, if you didn't do it, you don't have anything to worry about, right?"

"You mean apart from maybe being charged with murder and having my name dragged through the mud? Not exactly the sort of press coverage one wants while he's waiting to hear if he's going to be given the top slot."

"Yeah, I get that. So what do you think about the dog?"

"You really want him?"

"We do."

"After what you did to me at lunch, you can understand why I might not want to do something nice for you?"

"All I did was respond to your questions. It's not my fault you didn't like the answers," I said. "And don't forget, you were the one who flipped me off."

"Yeah, sorry about that," he said, laughing. "Force of habit. I used to do it to Middleton at least half a dozen times a day."

"I probably deserved it," I said, frowning as he ordered yet another scotch. "What do you say?"

"I'm still deciding," he said, giving me a sly smile. "But I'm leaning toward no."

"No? Why?"

"Because I really don't like you," he said, shrugging. "Don't get me wrong. I wouldn't kick you out of bed for eating dog biscuits, but you really don't *move the needle* if you get my drift."

"Got it. That's probably because you don't have any control over me."

He stared at me, seemed to be thinking hard about what I'd just said, and then nodded.

"I guess that could be it," he said, rattling his ice cubes. "But I'm sorry, it's gonna be a no on the dog."

"I see. Then you probably should know that my plan is to make sure that every media outlet I can find is going to hear about Jack. And I'll make sure to mention that you've hinted about putting the dog down."

"Oh, I'm shaking in my boots," he said, reaching for his fresh drink. "Why would any media outlet be interested in that story?"

"Because I personally witnessed how Middleton mistreated that dog. Animal cruelty stories always attract a lot of attention, especially one involving the largest chain of pet stores in North America. And even if the media isn't interested in the story, I'm willing to bet your shareholders and board of directors would be."

He set his drink down on the bar and gave me a look of admiration.

"Playing a little hardball," he said, nodding. "Well done. Well, I suppose it's not the best time to add any more *uncertainty* to the current situation. And there's no reason to bother our shareholders. Or the media. And certainly not the board. We're already talking about swapping the dog out for another animal to represent the brand."

"If I were you, I'd go with a snake," I said, pushing my half-full glass of wine away. "One of those really big ones that swallow things whole."

"There's no need to get snarky," he said, shaking his head. "Especially since you've just won the argument. Knock yourself out. Keep the dog." He reached into his wallet and handed me one of his cards. "Call my office. They'll arrange to get you all the dog's records."

"I'll do that," I said, glancing at the card. "Thanks. And good luck convincing the cops you didn't do it."

"I like my chances," he said, pounding his drink. "My prints didn't match the ones on the can of drain cleaner."

"That's gotta help."

"That's what I thought. But now the cops are insinuating that a guy in my position wouldn't have any problem finding someone to do it for him."

"You mean, like a personal lackey?"

"You really are relentless, aren't you?"

"I have my moments," I said, tossing my bag over my shoulder.

"It's been driving me crazy all day, but I'm sure we've met before," he said, squinting at me.

"We have. It was at a conference in Boston a couple of years ago. We were in the hotel bar, and you were putting on the full court press. Then you said the only thing that would make me hotter was if I had your money."

"Oh, yeah," he said, grimacing. "Now I remember. I used to use that line all the time. Amazing how many times it actually worked. If it's any consolation, I wouldn't have used it on you if I'd known you were rich."

"It's not," I said, shaking my head but still managing a small smile.

"So, you really are rich?"

"Yeah, I guess I am," I said, frowning.

"You guess?"

"I don't like to think about it."

"What on earth is the matter with you?"

"There are a lot of theories floating around about that."

"Yes, I'm sure there are," he said, laughing. "How much are you worth?"

I flinched at the question. Still getting used to saying it out loud, I leaned in and whispered the number in his ear. He flinched and stared at me.

"Wow. Really?"

"Give or take."

"Maybe I should flip that line around when I use it on you, huh?"

"No, don't waste your time. Having my money wouldn't make you any hotter. Unless you spent some of it on a soul."

"A soul? What the heck would I do with one of those?" he said, mocking me with a grin I immediately wanted to knock off his face. "Well, my offer stands. I think we could have a lot of fun together. If you change your mind, you know where to find me," he said, snapping his fingers to get the bartender's attention.

"Should be easy enough," I said, giving him a finger wave as I began walking away. "There can't be that many federal prisons."

Chapter 12

Josie, dressed in sweatpants and a tee shirt I'd given her with the slogan, *My therapist has four legs,* reached for the bag of bite-sized and shook her head at me.

"Use some of it to buy a soul?"

"Yeah," I said, shrugging. "Probably not my best effort."

"But you got him to agree to turn Jack over. Mission accomplished," she said, tossing a bite-sized into her mouth. Then she glanced over at the dog who was keeping a close eye on the action. "Sorry, Jack. No chocolate for you. Do you think Rollins was the one who killed Middleton?"

"I keep going back and forth on it," I said, frowning. "Right now, I'm leaning toward no." I caught her eye. "At one point, he asked me how much money I had."

"That was rude," Josie said, unwrapping another bite-sized. "Did you tell him?"

"I managed to whisper it in his ear."

"I guess that's some sort of breakthrough for you, huh?"

"Maybe. Mentioning it twice in one day must be some sort of record," I said, then shook my head. "I have to stop obsessing about it. It is what it is, right?"

"Yeah. It's just money."

"Exactly," I said, nodding.

"It's just that most of us use a wallet, while you need a tractor-trailer to carry your cash around."

"Not funny."

"Disagree," she said, glancing at her watch. "Ten past seven. She's late."

"That's not a good start," I said. "Interview rule number one; get there early."

As soon as I finished talking, we heard a soft knock. I hopped off the couch and headed for the door. I opened it, and a red-eyed Bobbie was standing in front of me. She appeared to be shaking, and I couldn't tell if she was afraid or simply angry. I stepped back, and she entered the suite and exhaled loudly.

"I'm so sorry I'm late," she said, literally wringing her hands. "I was headed for the elevator when the conference coordinator stopped me. Since the cops didn't find a match on any of the fingerprints, they decided to print all of the serving staff working that night. I offered to stop by after the interview, but they were adamant I had to do it right then. I'm so sorry. I can't believe I'm late for my own job interview."

"That's okay," I said, ushering her to one of the chairs that sat between the two couches. "You've been crying?"

"Yes," she said, wiping her eyes with a tissue.

"The cops made you cry?" Josie said, sitting up on the couch.

"No, my brother did," Bobbie said. "We had a big fight just before I left to come up here. And I was crying the whole time I was getting fingerprinted. The cops thought they were the reason and kept apologizing the whole time."

"The cops apologized?" I said, frowning.

"*Canadian* cops," Josie said.

"Sure, sure."

"I can't believe I'm late for the interview," Bobbie said, still trying to catch her breath.

"Well, you're here now," I said. "Do you want a glass of wine?"

"Is that a test?" she said, managing a small grin.

"No," I said, laughing. "Just an offer of a glass of wine. But it's nice to see you're paying attention."

"If you're having some, sure."

I poured three glasses and passed them around. I sat down on the couch. Jack decided he wanted a change of scenery, so he hopped up next to me and cocked his head as he stared at Bobbie.

"What were you and your brother fighting about?" Josie said.

"The possibility that I might be moving somewhere without him," she said, fighting back against another stream of tears. "He got mad and said some awful things to me."

"I'm sorry to hear that," Josie said. "But you two must be very close, right?"

"Most of the time," she said, shaking her head. "But he can be insufferable."

"Well, since you brought your brother up," I said, leaning forward. "Before we start the interview, there's something we need to discuss with you."

"You talked to Chef Claire, didn't you?" Bobbie said.

"Yes, as a matter of fact, we did," I said. "How did you know that?"

"You wouldn't hire the sister of her old boyfriend without checking with her first. Especially since you know that it didn't end well."

"Good answer," Josie said.

"What did she say?" Bobbie said, shifting nervously in her chair.

"She said if you could assure us that your brother won't be showing up in Clay Bay, she might be willing to give it a shot," I said.

Bobbie stared off at the far wall deep in thought.

"I think I can do that," she said, slowly. "It may take me a few days to get him to come around, but in the end, Charlie always tries to do everything he can to make me happy."

"Do you know anything about a restraining order?" Josie said.

"Yes, I do," Bobbie said, sighing. "Did Chef Claire go into any details about it?"

"No, not yet," I said.

"Then I'd like to let her explain what happened. If that's okay with you."

I glanced at Josie who nodded in agreement.

"Okay, fair enough," I said, glancing at Josie. "Weird situation, huh?"

"Weird's a word for it," she said, taking a sip of wine.

"It's sort of a first for me, too," Bobbie said, managing a smile.

"All right," I said, grabbing the resume off the table. "Let's get started. Your background looks great, and you've certainly demonstrated your dedication to animals."

"Thank you."

"But we do have a few questions about your pet grooming business that went under. Based on your resume, it sounds like it was very successful, and then it was gone. What happened?"

"It went under because of this," she said, reaching into her bag and removing a colorful, stuffed dog toy. "I'd like you to meet Wags. He was going to be the star, but that's also what I was going to call the company."

She tossed the toy to Josie who caught it and examined it. Jack went on point and gave the toy a loving stare.

"It's cute. And incredibly sturdy," she said, tossing it to me.

"Yeah, it looks like it could take a pounding. Even Captain might have a hard time destroying this one."

"Captain?" Bobbie said.

"My Newfie," Josie said. "He's known for being a bit of a bruiser."

I tossed the toy across the room, and Jack made a beeline for it. He snatched the toy up with his mouth and tussled with it emitting a low growl the entire time.

"I think he likes it," Josie said, laughing.

"Dogs love them," Bobbie said. "I came up with the idea and had a bunch of prototypes made. I was so sure the line of toys was going to be a hit, I sunk everything I had into it. And I thought I had everything in place for a bank loan, but then it fell through. So here I am. Schlepping food and drinks to conference goers. No offense."

"None taken," Josie said. "How many different toys did you have planned?"

"A ton," she said, shrugging. "You probably saw on my resume that my background is in art design. But I was having a hard time finding a job in the fashion industry. So I decided to give the grooming business a shot. And one day I was shampooing this cute little beagle when the idea just hit me. Do you remember Beanie Babies?"

"Sure," Josie said. "I was really into collecting them for a while."

"And then she discovered food."

"Shut it."

"My plan was to do the same thing, but for dogs. Well, for their owners, actually," she said. "I was going to introduce a new toy every month in a small, medium, and large size. Do you have any idea how much money people spend on their dogs?"

"Yeah, we could probably ballpark it," Josie deadpanned.

"Duh," Bobbie said, embarrassed. "Look who I'm talking to."

Lightbulbs exploded in my head, and I glanced over at Jack who was on his back with the toy in his mouth.

"All the banks turned you down?" I said.

"Yeah, but not right away," she said. "Eventually, they all said I didn't have the necessary track record to pull off something like this. It seemed like a no-brainer to me. But I guess I wasn't lucky enough to find a banker who had any vision and was a dog lover."

"And you had a business plan?" I said.

"I have a great business plan," she said, managing a sad laugh. "Just no money. Oh, well. Live and learn, right?"

"Did you patent the idea?" I said, glancing at Josie who was beaming at me.

"Patents, trademarks, copyright. You name it. I got it. A lot of good they did me. Talk about throwing money down the drain."

"It sounds like you put an awful lot of work into this," I said.

"Three years," Bobbie said, scowling. "And here I am, still trying to dig out."

126

"I'm sorry you had to go through all of that, Bobbie," I said. "But I'm afraid I have some more bad news for you."

"You do?"

"Yes. I'm sorry, but I have to say that you aren't the person we want running our rescue program."

"I'm not," she said, crushed.

"No," Josie said. "Definitely not."

"But why not?" she said, starting to tear up.

"Don't get me wrong. I'm sure you'd do a great job, but that would be a complete waste of your talents," I said, unable to contain my grin. "We want you running Wags."

"What?" she said, stunned as she glanced back and forth at us.

"It's an amazing idea," I said. "Dog people will snatch these things up."

"They certainly will," Josie said. "You know, in addition to the usual distribution outlets, we could also sell them online by subscription, and each month a new toy would arrive in the mail."

"I was thinking the same thing," Bobbie said.

"You know who'd be perfect for the online side of the business?" I said, glancing at Josie.

"Sammy."

"Exactly," I said.

"You're serious about funding my idea? You'd want to go into business with me?"

"If the business plan looks anything like you say it does," I said. "I have to say that it's a distinct possibility."

"I'm not worried about that. The business plan is solid. How big a role would you want?"

"Well, we sure don't want to run it," Josie said, shaking her head. "We've got more than enough on our plate at the moment."

"No kidding. And my aversion to all things corporate is well known," I said, laughing. "Don't worry, you'd keep majority control."

"But how would it work?" Bobbie said, leaning forward in her chair.

"I have no idea," I said, shrugging. "We usually just start talking until we come up with something everybody can agree to."

"And if we can't all agree, we don't do it," Josie said.

"Off the top of my head, you'd probably keep at least sixty percent, what's left would go to the three of us," I said.

"Three?" Bobbie said.

"Chef Claire," Josie said.

"You'd include Chef Claire?"

"Absolutely," I said. "We're sort of like the three musketeers."

"And she feeds us very well," Josie said, laughing. "You can't put a price on that."

"I have the business plan and some more of the prototypes down in my car," Bobbie said. "Should I go get them?"

"I don't see why not," I said.

"I'd love to see them," Josie said, glancing at Jack who was once again tussling with the toy. "But I don't like your chances of getting that one back."

Bobbie raced out the door. I sunk back into the couch deep in thought.

"A dog toy business," Josie said. "I like it."

"Yeah, and I really like the collectible angle. I think it could be big."

"But that's not why you did it."

"What do you mean?"

"You were looking for a way to help her, and, at the same time, not give Chef Claire any reason to freak out."

"Maybe," I said, giving her a coy smile.

"And since she won't be running our rescue program, there's no reason for her to move to Clay Bay."

"No, there isn't. Funny how things work out, huh? Besides, locating the company here will give us a good reason to visit Ottawa. We both love it here."

"We do," Josie said. "Well, I will give you this, my friend. There's never a dull moment when you're around."

"Compliment?"

"Maybe," Josie said, reaching for the bag of bite-sized.

"There's just one thing that's bothering me," I said, frowning.

"That you're turning into your mother?"

"Yeah. This is exactly the sort of thing she would do."

"Doing well by doing good," Josie said. "There's nothing wrong with that."

"No, there's not," I said. "Knowing her, she'll want in on the deal." Then I chuckled. "But we couldn't do that to Bobbie."

Josie snorted and tossed me the bag of bite-sized.

"This could be a lot of fun," Josie said, glancing over at Jack who was pushing the toy across the carpet with his nose. "And maybe she'll name one of the toys after me."

"Snacker?"

"Funny."

Chapter 13

Josie headed for the breakfast buffet while I swung by registration to request a late checkout. The police had finally let us know there was no need for us to change our original plans, and we decided to head for home as soon as possible that afternoon. The conference was scheduled to wrap up at noon right after the morning sessions, but there was no way I had time to attend any of them. My to-do list was longer than I would have liked, and I knew I'd have to maintain my focus if we were going to be able to fit in lunch at Mandarin then get on the road by two.

I got our checkout time moved back an hour then left the registration desk to join Josie. On the way, I crossed paths with Marjorie and her son. Marjorie, while less stressed than she'd been earlier in the conference, obviously still had a lot on her mind, and she almost walked right past me.

"Marjorie," I said.

"Oh, Suzy, hello," she said, coming to a sudden stop. "I didn't even see you. How are you?"

"I'm good. Hi, Thomas."

"Hi."

He barely made eye contact. I guess he was still mad at me for suggesting he might have been the one who killed Middleton. I made a mental note to figure out a way to make it up to him, then decided I better write it down. I added the item to my to-do list then focused on his mother.

"I just wanted to thank you again for inviting us," I said.

"No, thank you. Your session was wonderful. In fact, several people have already suggested that we have you back next year," Marjorie said, shifting several large folders she was carrying to her other arm.

"You're going to do it again?" I said, grinning. "You are a glutton for punishment."

"That's what my husband said," she said, laughing.

"Let me hold those for you, Mom," Thomas said, reaching for the stack of folders.

"Okay, but don't drop them," she said, reluctantly handing them over.

Thomas, mildly annoyed at his mother, shook his head but said nothing. Then he pointed in the direction of the breakfast buffet.

"I'm going to head on in," he said. "I'll save you a seat."

"Thanks. I'll be there in a minute."

We watched him walk away.

"He's still mad at me, isn't he?"

"Maybe a little," Marjorie said, staring after her son. "Don't worry, he'll get over it. You just caught him by surprise."

"Yeah, I have a tendency to do that," I said, frowning.

"And to be honest, I think he's got a bit of a crush on you."

"Really? My radar must be on the fritz," I said. "Look, I'm glad I ran into you. I'm wondering if you've seen the guy who punched Middleton the other night."

"Are you talking about Victor Rollins?"

"No, I already spoke with him. And that was a half-hour of my life I'll never get back. I'm talking about the other guy. There was a woman tugging at his shirt trying to hold him back."

"That was his wife, Rena," Marjorie said. "His name is Harold Smythe. They left the conference yesterday."

"I see. Do you know them?"

"Yes, fairly well. Harold is a venture capitalist, and I believe he's done some things with Middleton in the past," she said, raising an eyebrow at me. "But that's not why he was angry."

"Oh, goodie," I said, laughing. "I knew there had to be a story there somewhere."

"Yes," she said, inching closer and lowering her voice. "Rena and Middleton have been having a rather torrid affair. At least they were."

"And then Harold found out and didn't take the news well."

"Nothing gets by you," Marjorie said, laughing. "No, not well at all. But the police cleared them of the murder yesterday. After Harold punched Middleton, Rena dragged him off to the lobby, and they spent close to an hour arguing near the reception desk. Dozens of witnesses, including several of the hotel staff, confirmed it."

"Well, that saves me some time," I said out loud to myself as I crossed the item off my to-do list.

"What's that?"

"Oh, nothing. Have you spoken with the police lately?"

"It seems like that's all I've been doing," she said. "They're constantly asking me questions about some of the attendees. Including you and Josie, by the way."

"Yeah, I know. We talked to them the other night. They started off a little huffy, but they settled down after we dropped a few comments about their mutual *liaison*."

"Really?"

"Yeah," I said, nodding. "He probably should have taken off his wedding ring."

"What is it about conferences that bring out that sort of behavior?"

"Distance from home and an open bar would be my guess. Are the cops still around?"

"I'm sure they are," she said, frowning as she looked across the lobby. "Perfect."

I followed her eyes and saw Roxanne standing next to a man near the front door. She had one hand on his arm and was waving at me with the other. I returned the wave and focused on Marjorie who was now glaring at the couple.

"Do you know Roxanne?" I said.

"Only by reputation."

"She's not wasting any time," I said, shaking my head.

"No, apparently not."

"Do you know who the guy is?"

"My husband," she said, giving me a small goodbye wave as she strode across the lobby.

I watched Marjorie exchange a few pointed comments with her husband, then dismiss Roxanne with a wave of her hand. Roxanne did her best walk as she crossed the lobby toward me.

"What's got into her?" she said, coming to a stop next to me.

"I'm sure she has a lot on her mind," I said, doing my best not to laugh.

"Well, that was just rude," Roxanne said. "It's not like I was trying to sleep with the guy. All I wanted was a phone number."

"You wanted his phone number?"

"No, a friend of his I spent the night with. The guy managed to slip out this morning without giving it to me. I hate when that happens."

"I'm sure you'll track him down," I said, shaking my head at her. "That's why you never came back to the suite?"

"Yeah, I went to one of the hotel restaurants and saw this guy eating by himself. I told him he looked lonely, and he asked me to join him. Then he told me his whole life story over dinner. And the rest, as they say, is history."

"What does he do?"

"Pretty much what every other man I date does."

"Spends money on you?" I said, laughing.

"Exactly," she said, nodding. "Or at least I thought he was going to." She fished through her purse and pulled out a valet parking ticket. "I gotta get going."

"Where are you off to?"

"Montreal. There's an investment conference starting tomorrow."

"You're going to an investment conference?"

"Yeah. Some of the richest people on the planet are supposed to be there so I thought I'd do a little shopping," she said, then paused to make eye contact. "You'd probably call it hunting."

"Tomato, tomahto."

"Try not to judge me, Suzy," she snapped, brushing her hair back from her face. "We all make our choices. Mine is to find a rich husband before it's too late. And the clock is definitely ticking."

"I like your chances, Roxanne. You seem both focused and persistent."

"Oh, don't worry, I'm tenacious," she said, laughing. "And let me know if you're ever in the mood to do a little hunting. We'd make a pretty good team. They wouldn't know what hit them."

"Thanks, but I'm pretty busy with the dogs," I said, shrugging.

"Yeah," she said, her voice dropping to a reverential whisper. "You guys do really good work. You should be proud of that." Then her mood brightened again, and she beamed at me. "Well, I need to get going. Wish me luck. And thanks again for helping me out the other night."

Then she was gone. I watched her strut across the lobby, have a quick chat with the doorman that ended with a peck on the cheek, and then she headed outside and climbed into a new Mercedes and drove off. I crossed off saying goodbye to Roxanne from my to-do list and counted my blessings as I turned to head for the breakfast buffet.

"Excuse me, are you Ms. Chandler?"

I stopped and waited as one of the registration clerks approach me carrying a thick envelope.

"Yes, that's me," I said, nodding at the envelope. "Is that for me?"

"Yes, it just came by courier. I believe it's from Middleton Enterprises," the clerk said, handing it over.

"That was quick," I said, accepting the envelope. "Thanks."

I wasn't sure about the protocol but tipped him anyway. He glanced down at the bill, pleasantly surprised, then gave me a quick salute as he walked away. I opened the envelope and removed several documents, all of them dealing with Jack. I confirmed his vaccination records were up to date, glanced briefly at his lineage, then slid all of them back inside the envelope. I tucked the envelope under one arm and crossed the item off my list.

"What the heck are you doing hanging out in the lobby?"

I glanced over my shoulder and saw Josie approaching gently rubbing her stomach.

"Making incredible progress. You won't believe how much I'm getting done. Who knew all I had to do was stand around here? People are just finding me," I said. "How was breakfast?"

"It was great, but I probably should have stopped after my first stack of pancakes," she said, stifling a burp. "What's that?"

"Jack's papers," I said, handing her the envelope. "He's all set. We shouldn't have any problems going back across the border."

"Impressive lineage," she said, scanning the documents. "He's a rock star."

I gave her a quick summary of the last twenty minutes, and she listened carefully. I finished, then had a thought.

"Is Bobbie still watching Jack?"

"Yeah, she just took him for a walk."

"Don't forget that we need to schedule a time for her to come to Clay Bay for the four of us to talk," I said, glancing down at my to-do list.

"Already done," Josie said. "She stopped by while I was eating, and we talked about it. She's coming over on Monday. I thought family dinner night would be a good time to do it."

"Perfect," I said, then paused. "I already invited Chief Abrams to dinner. Do you think that's going to be a problem?"

"No, we'll eat first," Josie said. "And then he can take off, or stick around and play with the dogs."

"Yeah, that'll work," I said, crossing the item off my list.

"What do you have left to do?" she said, peering at my list.

"Have a chat with those two cops," I said, shrugging. "That's it."

"Don't forget lunch at the Mandarin," she said.

"Really? You're already thinking about lunch?"

"I've been thinking about it since we got here," she said, shrugging. "I just saw the cops heading toward the conference registration area."

"Then that's where I'm heading," I said, sliding my bag onto my other shoulder. "You want to come along?"

"No, I'm gonna check out a couple of the morning sessions," she said. "I'll meet you by the front door at eleven-thirty. Try not to annoy the cops too much."

"I thought I might ask them if they want to join us for lunch," I said, slipping my to-do list into my pocket. "You know, get them out of their element. Maybe they'll relax and feel like chatting."

Josie stared at me in disbelief, then shook her head and walked away.

"Hey," I said, calling after her. "Cops gotta eat, too."

Chapter 14

Just before noon I parked in front of the restaurant and glanced over my shoulder into the backseat.

"You think Jack will be okay staying out here in the car while we eat?" I said, glancing at Josie.

Josie turned around in her seat to look at the dog that was nestled on a stack of blankets and a thick pillow. He had a paw draped over the toy Bobbie had given him and was snoring loudly. Josie turned back around in her seat and nodded.

"Yeah, I think he'll be fine," she said, laughing.

I cracked all the windows, felt the cool fall breeze, then hopped out and locked the car just as the unmarked police car pulled in next to us. Bill and Shirley, wearing plainclothes today, got out and stretched in unison.

"You made it," I said.

"A free lunch at Mandarin?" Bill said. "Probably not something we're gonna say no to."

"Now remember what I told you," I said, nodding my head at Josie. "Just keep your distance when she picks up her knife and fork. And *never* sneak up behind her when she's eating."

"Shut it. And for the record, I won't be using a knife and fork."

"You're going with chopsticks?" I said, heading for the front door.

"What else would I use at a Chinese restaurant?"

"I don't know. Maybe a shovel," I said, shrugging as I held the door open for everyone.

"Feel free to just go ahead and shoot her," Josie said to the two cops as she stepped inside.

She came to a stop and stared lovingly at the long display of dishes that easily exceeded a hundred items. A huge smile appeared on her face, and she softly clapped her hands.

"It's like that famous toy store in New York," she said.

"What?"

"The toy store that was in all those movies," she said, glancing at me. "I think it closed a couple of years ago."

"Are you talking about F.A.O. Schwarz?"

"That's the one," she said. "This place is the F.A.O. Schwarz of Chinese food."

I glanced at Bill and Shirley who were obviously confused and perhaps reconsidering their decision to join us. Josie grabbed a plate and gave us an onward-ho wave. We followed at a safe distance, filled our plates, then found an empty table in the dining room. We ate in silence for several minutes, apart from the grunts and groans the food produced, then Josie put down her chopsticks and frowned.

"What's the matter?" I said, glancing over at her.

"I forgot to grab one of the Eggs Benedict," she said. "Remind me to get one on my next trip."

"They have Eggs Benedict?" I said, glancing back toward the buffet tables.

"Yeah, but you wouldn't like it. Instead of Canadian bacon, they substitute smoked salmon."

"Yuk," I said. "Why would they do something dumb like that and ruin a perfect dish?"

"I think it's the work of a genius," she said, then had a thought and glanced over at the cops. "Hey, I've been wondering about something. On this side of the border, do you guys call it Canadian bacon, or just bacon?"

"I think we're pretty flexible on that one," Bill said, still baffled by mealtime Josie.

I washed down a particularly spicy mouthful of Kung Pao chicken with a gulp of water and focused on the two cops who were sitting across the table.

"I heard you cleared Harold and Rena Smythe," I said casually as I speared a piece of broccoli.

"We did," Bill said, staring at me.

If he was curious about where I'd heard that bit of information, he let it pass without asking.

"Yeah," Shirley said, slowly chewing her food. "The only people those two might kill would be each other."

"I guess affairs tend to have that effect on some people," I said, smiling as I glanced back and forth at them. Then I flinched when I felt Josie kick me under the table. "But what the heck. We're all adults here, right?"

"Yeah, we're all adults," Bill said, giving me a dark stare.

"How long have you two been partners?" I said, trying to turn the mood around.

"Three years," Shirley said.

"Three years, one month, and four days," Bill said, beaming at his partner.

Shirley grinned, pushed her hair back from her face, and reached for the soy sauce. I glanced over at Bill's left hand and saw his wedding ring. I must have flinched because he noticed my reaction and put his chopsticks down.

"Yes?" he said, folding his hands in front of him on the table.

"Nothing. It's none of my business," I said, red-faced.

"No, it's not," he said, tearing up. "But I should probably tell you that I'm a widower."

Shirley reached over and placed her hand on his.

"I'm just having a really hard time taking the ring off," he said, picking up his chopsticks.

"You'll get there," Shirley said. "Take all the time you need."

"Well, don't I feel like a total jerk," I said, frowning.

"Don't worry about it," he said. "It's a logical assumption to make."

"I'm so sorry," I said.

"It's okay," Shirley said, patting his hand. "Him wearing that ring is about the only thing that keeps us from tearing off each other's clothes at work."

"You're so good to me," Bill said, going in for a kiss that made me blush. It lasted long enough to get Josie to look up from the crab leg she was doing battle with. Eventually, they broke contact, and Shirley laughed.

"I told you not to eat all those oysters," she said, squeezing his arm.

"They have oysters?" Josie said, glancing over at his plate. "How the heck did I miss them?"

"We had them last night," Bill said.

"Oh, I thought I was slipping there for a moment," Josie said, resuming her attack on the crab leg.

I was about to ask my next question when a piece of crab shell landed on the side of my face. I picked it off and tossed it back on her plate, then glared at her.

"Oops," she said, suppressing a giggle. "Incoming."

"What's next for the investigation?" I said to the lovebird cops.

"We've sort of hit an impasse," Shirley said. "We're not sure where we're going to take it."

"But you like Rollins for it, don't you?" I said casually as I picked my way around a shrimp in my fried rice I'd taken my mistake.

"I'm not sure we should be talking about this with you, Suzy," Bill said, glancing at his partner.

"Sure, sure. I get that," I said, pausing as Josie got up to make a return trip to the buffet. "Although I don't think he did it, Rollins seems to be the only logical suspect at the moment. Unless there's additional evidence I'm not aware of."

Both cops stared at me. I wanted to believe it was because I was demonstrating amazing detective abilities, but I imagine they were staring because they were having a hard time dealing with my intrusive behavior. Eventually, Bill softened and nodded at me.

"Yes, we can confirm that Rollins is high on our list. So far," he said, shrugging.

"But you don't have it," I said, leaning forward and putting my elbows on the table.

"Have what?" Shirley said.

"Enough evidence to arrest him."

"No, we don't," she said, sliding a piece of grilled fish into her mouth.

I did my best not to grimace at what I considered one of the most disgusting things anybody could eat. I grabbed a piece of orange chicken with my chopsticks to take my mind off it and chewed slowly before continuing.

"You know, it's the timing of events that point to him," I said. "That's what I can't shake."

"Timing of what events?" Bill said, leaning forward.

"The fact that Middleton got killed the same day he told Rollins that he was going to do some restructuring and make some drastic changes to his job responsibilities."

Both cops stared at me with their mouths open, and it eventually dawned on me that they didn't have a clue what I was talking about. When he called earlier this morning, Chief Abrams had told me that the news about the changes Middleton was about to implement hadn't gone public, but I hadn't even considered the possibility that the two bewildered cops sitting across the table from me hadn't heard about it. I kicked myself under the table and hoped that I hadn't put Chief Abrams or his buddy at the SEC in a difficult spot.

"Drastic changes to his job?" Shirley said.

"Yeah."

"That's news to us," Bill said. "Would you mind explaining where you heard it?"

"It came from somebody at the SEC," I said, shrugging, then felt the need to clarify. "The one that tries to keep an eye on the financial industry, not the football conference."

"Got it," Bill said, unable to stop staring at me.

"That slimeball Rollins never said a word about it," Shirley said to her partner. "It certainly provides more than enough motive."

"Yes, it certainly does," Bill said, then focused on me. "What specifically did you hear?"

"Not a lot, really," I said. "But Middleton Enterprises is going to miss its quarterly numbers, and a couple of regions Rollins has direct responsibility for are in the tank. Middleton was blaming Rollins for the bad quarter and using it as the reason to restructure his job."

"It's not enough," Shirley said. "We still can't place him at the scene."

"He had help," Bill said, his voice rising a notch. "That has to be it."

"So we're back to that," Shirley said, shaking her head. "I really don't think it's possible, Bill."

"Sure it was," he said. "Especially if he'd been planning it for a long time. Maybe hearing about what was happening to his job was the last straw."

"No, I don't like it," Shirley said, shaking her head.

"Me either," I said, out loud to myself.

"I'm sorry," Bill said, annoyed. "But I don't remember asking you for your opinion."

"Yeah, I really need to work on that. But I have to agree with Shirley on this one, Bill. The murder has the look of a spontaneous act brought on by sudden rage. From what I've seen, Rollins is very calculating. I don't think he even goes to the bathroom without a strategy."

Bill picked at his food, then sat back in his chair. Josie returned with a fresh plate piled high.

"I love this place," she said, reaching for her chopsticks. Then she picked up on the silence at the table. "Did I miss something?"

"No," I said. "We were just debating whether or not Rollins is the murderer."

"It sounds like it's a moot point at the moment," she said with a shrug as she dug into her second helping.

"How so?" Shirley said.

Josie chewed, then swallowed and wiped her mouth. "No match on the fingerprints, no witnesses, and no traces of Middleton's blood on Rollins. We all saw how badly the guy was bleeding from his nose. It would have been impossible to pour drain cleaner down the guy's throat and not get some blood on you." She slowly chewed a chunk of chicken then sipped water. "You can't go into court with that case. His lawyers would have a field day."

"She's right," Shirley said.

"Yes, and that's why we haven't arrested him. But I still like him for the murder," Bill said, then glared at me. "I really wish you wouldn't look at me like that."

"Like what?" I said.

"Like I'm an idiot," he said.

"Sorry. I just don't see Rollins doing it."

Bill calmed down and picked at his food. "The lack of blood does bother me. Not to mention that we can't match the prints. We must have fingerprinted five hundred people."

"You did find blood on one person," Josie said, casually tossing it out.

"Roxanne?" Shirley said. "She's the one who found the body. And since she'd been engaged to the guy, it makes sense that she would have tried to comfort him."

"Maybe," Josie said.

"Where are you going with this?" I said, glancing over at her.

"I'm not going anywhere. I'm just reviewing some of the facts."

"Middleton was Roxanne's meal ticket," I said, frowning. "Why on earth would she want to kill him?"

"I'm not saying she did," Josie said. "I'm saying that maybe he was trying to kill her."

A stunned silence fell over the table.

"What on earth are you talking about?" I said.

"Did you find Middleton's prints on the can of drain cleaner?" Josie said, smashing open another crab leg that went everywhere.

"Yes, as a matter of fact, we did," Bill said. "They were consistent with someone who was trying to fend off an attack." He raised his hands in front of his face to demonstrate what he was talking about.

"But couldn't he also have been trying to pour it on someone else?" she said, wiping my cheek with her napkin. "Sorry about that." Then she focused on the cops. "Was the location of the prints also consistent with someone who might have been on the attack as opposed to trying to defend himself?"

Bill and Shirley glanced at each other. Eventually, they shrugged.

"Yeah, I guess it's possible," he said. "But that's kind of a stretch."

"It explains the blood," Josie said, rubbing her stomach. "I'm such a little piggy."

"But it still doesn't explain the lack of fingerprints," Shirley said.

Josie set her chopsticks down and wiped her mouth again.

"If you came at me with a can of drain cleaner," she said. "I would undoubtedly do everything I could to stop you, right?"

"Well, sure," Shirley said.

"And instead of reaching for the can, wouldn't it be plausible for me to try to grab your arms to stop you?"

"Yes, I can see that," Bill said, nodding.

"And if Roxanne did grab his arms, that wouldn't necessarily leave any prints."

"Maybe not," Bill said.

"And even if it did, knowing Roxanne the way we do, I imagine you'd find her prints all over his body," she said, grinning.

"Now that's funny," Shirley said, grinning back at Josie. "You two do have some bad history, don't you?"

"Maybe a bit," she conceded with a shrug.

I snorted.

"Shut it."

"Did you really stab her?" Shirley said.

"Only on the hand," Josie snapped. "And it was an accident."

"Why would Middleton want to kill Roxanne?" I said.

"Maybe he was already bored with her," Josie said. "We know he was sleeping with other women. Maybe he eventually woke up and decided he didn't want to give away a bunch of money in a divorce. Who knows?"

"No," I said, shaking my head. "I don't like Roxanne for it at all. Even in self-defense."

"Well, it's better than anything you've got," Josie said, laughing.

"That's not hard to do," I said, shrugging. "I got nothing."

"There you go," she said, gently punching me on the shoulder.

"It's an interesting theory," Bill said. "I guess we could take another look at it through that lens."

"Yeah, we can do that," Shirley said. "But I gotta agree with Suzy. I don't see it."

"Well, something has to break soon, or this is going to end up as one of those cases that never get solved."

"Oh, I hate when that happens," I said, then flushed with embarrassment when I saw the look the two cops were giving me. "I mean, you guys must hate it when that happens."

"Yeah, it's a real drag," Bill said, laughing as he tossed his napkin on the table. "We should get going. Thanks so much for lunch. This has been, to say the least, most interesting."

"Yes, thanks so much," Shirley said, standing. "It was delicious."

"Aren't you going to stay for dessert?" Josie said, frowning at them.

"Dessert?" Bill said. "You must be joking."

"I never joke about dessert."

They both laughed, and Bill glanced over at me.

"If your contact at the SEC happens to come up with anything else, we'd appreciate it if you let us know."

"Will do," I said. "Good luck with it."

They waved and headed outside.

"Nice people," I said. "And they make a cute couple."

"Yes, they do," Josie said, getting up out of her chair. "You ready for the dessert table?"

"Yeah, I think I saved enough room."

I followed her toward the long line of desserts on display.

"You really think Roxanne killed Middleton in self-defense?"

"No," she said, slowing down as she approached an interesting collection of custards.

"But you just thought you'd float the idea?"

"Pretty much."

"Because you don't like Roxanne and wanted to drag her back into it?"

"No, that's not it. In her own way, I guess she's okay."

"Then why bring it up?"

"It's an alternate theory," she said, making eye contact with me. "And that's what was needed."

"Really?" I said, offended.

"Yes, you're way off your game on this one. And I'm getting tired of listening to you prattle on and on about some possible scenario that isn't holding water. Either come up with a new theory or let it go. You're driving me nuts."

"I'm stuck."

"No kidding," she said, coming to a sudden stop. "Oooh, custard-stuffed chocolate eclairs. Be still my beating heart."

"Maybe just one," I said, grabbing a small plate. "Roxanne might have done it in self-defense? When you think about it, it's not as crazy as it sounds."

Josie shook her head as she grabbed two of the eclairs.

"Why do I even bother?"

Chapter 15

We were on the road heading for home just after two; full, tired, and very much looking forward to seeing the dogs. Traffic was light once we got out of the city and hit Highway 416 heading south. About an hour later we were approaching the Custom and Immigration station at Ogdensburg. The agents took their time with us and used Jack as an excuse to linger. They reached through the rear windows to pet him and scratch his ears, all the while casually flirting with us. We let it play out, too tired to banter with them, and they eventually waved us through. We headed southwest, connected with Route 12, and made it home just as the sun was beginning to set.

Jack perked up immediately when I parked in front of the Inn, and he trotted at our heels as we went up the steps and through the front door. He stopped in the doorway, sniffed the air, and gave the place the once-over. I scooped him up in my arms and approached the registration counter where Sammy and Jill were beaming at the Jack Russell.

"Can't you guys go anywhere without getting another dog?" Sammy said, grinning as he took Jack from me. "He's gorgeous. Is he just visiting or is he a new member of the family?"

"He's officially one of us," Josie said, rubbing the dog's head. She tossed the envelope containing all his records on the counter. "We'll need to add all the important stuff into the computer and put the originals in the safe with the others when you get a chance. Oh, and he has a chip so let's make sure we update his record with…listen to me, you know the drill. I'll stop talking now."

"You got it," Sammy said, handing the dog to Jill.

"Thanks, Sammy," Josie said, stifling a yawn.

"Where did you get him?" Jill said, admiring the Jack Russell.

"You're looking at the former brand representative for Middleton Enterprises," I said, leaning against the counter.

"Really?" Jill said. "What's his name?"

"Jack," I said.

"That makes sense," Jill said, nodding.

"I probably would have gone with Russell," Josie said.

"He's amazing," Jill said. "How on earth did you get your hands on him?"

"Yeah," Sammy said, laughing as he glanced up from the keyboard. "What did you do, kill his owner?"

"No, somebody else beat us to it," Josie said.

"You're joking, right?" Jill said, staring at Josie.

"I wish," she said, glancing around the reception area. "How are things around here?"

"Things are great," Sammy said. "Everybody just had dinner, and I'm about to take them outside so they can do their business. How was the conference?"

"Eventful," Josie said. "We'll tell you all about it later. Is Chef Claire around?"

"No, she left for the restaurant a few minutes ago," Jill said. "But she said she wanted to talk to you as soon as possible after you got back. Is she doing okay? She's been in a really weird mood the past few days."

"She'll be fine," I said, glancing around. "Where are all the house dogs?"

"Chef Claire fed them up there, then took them outside. I'm sure they're all dying to see you."

"Works for me," I said, then looked at Josie. "What do you say we head up to the house and say hi to the dogs, then head to C's?"

"Sounds great," Josie said, then looked at Sammy and Jill. "Would you guys mind getting Jack socialized with some of the other dogs before you find a condo for him? He's going to be a bit disoriented for a day or two. Let's make sure he knows he's among friends."

"Sure," Sammy said. "He seems really subdued for a Jack Russell."

"Yeah, that's something we're going to need to work on with him," I said. "He's had a rough go of it."

"He hasn't been abused, has he?" Jill said, frowning.

156

"Well, he certainly hasn't been treated anywhere close to our standards. But he'll get his spirit back. And thanks again for taking such good care of the place. We'll see you guys in the morning."

We headed up to the house, spent over an hour getting reacquainted with Captain and Chloe and Chef Claire's Goldens, Al and Dente, then showered and headed for C's. We entered through the back door that led directly into the kitchen and glanced around for Chef Claire. The skeleton kitchen staff we retained on a year-round basis was dealing with the handful of order slips and not having to break much of a sweat doing it. A staff member saw us and pointed at the chef's table in the back of the kitchen where Chef Claire was sitting sipping coffee and staring off into space.

"Hey," she said, glancing at us when we sat down at the table. "How did the conference finish up?"

"With lunch at Mandarin," Josie said.

"Good call," Chef Claire said, giving us a half-hearted nod. "I hear that place is amazing."

"Are you okay?" I said, making room for a staff member as he approached with a pot of coffee and mugs for us. "Thanks, Carl." I added creamer and stirred my coffee without taking my eyes off her. "Hello. Earth to Chef Claire."

"Sorry," she said, shaking her head as if clearing away some cobwebs. "Charlie called again today. I'm afraid we may have to rethink the idea of hiring Bobbie."

"I think we have a solution to that," I said.

I launched into our idea for the dog toy business, and she listened carefully. When I finished, she sat back in her chair sipping her coffee.

"Bobbie wouldn't need to move here?" Chef Claire said.

"No, we'd base the company out of Ottawa," I said.

"But why would you include me as a partner?" she said, frowning. "I don't know anything about running a business like that."

"We didn't know anything about running a restaurant," Josie said. "But that didn't stop you from including us as your partners."

"Yeah, but this is different," Chef Claire said.

"No, it's not," I said, squeezing her hand. "Don't worry, you aren't going to have to do any of the work. Except for maybe testing out some new toys with Al and Dente. You'll hear more about it on Monday night when Bobbie joins us for family dinner."

"Just her, right?" Chef Claire said, nervously glancing back and forth at us.

"Of course," Josie said.

Chef Claire stared off, jiggling one leg nervously as she drummed her fingers on the table.

"What on earth did that guy do to you?"

She made eye contact and continued to stare at us, tight-lipped, for a long time. Then she nodded and slowly began to tell the tale of her experiences with Charlie. Josie and I listened closely and did our best not to interrupt, but we shared several looks of shock and surprise as she recited the history of her ill-fated relationship.

"When I got out of college, I applied for several engineering jobs, but I kept washing out during the interviews. And I finally realized I was sabotaging myself because I had no desire to be an engineer. So I decided to go to culinary school and ended up in L.A. It was a two-year program, and right after I started, I met Charlie. We connected right away, and since neither one of us had much money, we decided to get a two-bedroom apartment together and share expenses. Within a week, we realized that we weren't going to need the second bedroom, except for maybe storage. If you get my drift."

"Yeah, we got it," I said, nodding.

"And it was great at first," she said, brushing her hair back from her face. "Amazing, actually. He was sweet, attentive, and seemed to be the first guy who really got what I was all about. The first four months were the best I'd ever had with a new guy. But then something happened that changed things in a hurry." She glanced around the kitchen, decided the staff had everything under control, then continued. "We had a class assignment to prepare a seven-course meal worthy of the British aristocracy," she said, laughing and shaking her head. "It was something straight out of Downton Abbey. And my assigned partner was this guy from Alabama who was a total goofball and funny as all get out. We were laughing the whole time, and ended up tossing chunks of pastry dough at each other when we were making the Beef Wellington." She paused and looked at Josie.

"What?" Josie said, confused.

"I was expecting a comment from you," she said, laughing. "Didn't you hear me say Beef Wellington?"

"I heard you," Josie said. "But you refuse to make it, so why I should bother oohing and aahing about something I'm not going to get a chance to eat?"

"Well, you're about to find out why I don't make it anymore," Chef Claire said. "My partner and I were having a great time, and each course came out perfect, but Charlie just kept glaring at us the whole time."

"Jealous?"

"Turns out, insanely so. To this day, he refuses to call it what it is. He refers to it simply as an *overly protective* instinct," Chef Claire said, dismissing the idea with a smirk. "Even though he didn't say anything, I could tell he was really mad. And after he finished his assignment he left. I assumed he went home, but it turned out he was waiting for the guy outside by his car. And then Charlie jumped him and almost beat him to death. The poor guy was in the hospital for a month, and Charlie *almost* went to jail. But he got one-year probation."

"He beat him up just for having some laughs with you?" I said.

"Pretty much. That should have been enough for me to call it quits," Chef Claire said, exhaling loudly. "But being the rescuer I am, I had to hang in there. He promised it wouldn't happen again, I forgave him, blah, blah, blah…and the wheels on the bus go round and round."

"But it happened again, right?" I said.

"Yes, well, it was sort of the same thing. But not for a year and a half," she said. "Things changed after the first incident, and we were never quite the same. We stayed together, but, for me, I knew it was just temporary until we finished school. But I never had the guts to tell him that."

"That's probably because you were scared what he might do," Josie said.

"Yeah, that's what I tell myself," she said, sniffling back emotion. "But that was my big mistake. The longer I stayed with him, the more we argued. And because we always managed to get through it, the more convinced he became that we could survive anything. Instead of working on his control and anger issues, he got worse. And he started to smother me with questions and insinuations. Started following me around every time I hung out with anybody other than him. Even going out for coffee with a couple of girlfriends got to be a problem. Then the second thing happened."

Josie and I continued to lean forward hanging on every word.

"What did he do?" Josie whispered.

161

"Just before we were going to graduate culinary school, two of my girlfriends invited me to join them for a weekend in Vegas to celebrate."

"And he followed you there and made a scene?" I said, frowning.

"Worse. Just before I headed to the airport, he locked me in our bedroom at the apartment. He'd put a special lock on the window, he took my phone, and even put a chain across the door."

"Wow," Josie whispered. "That's insane."

"That's the word for it," Chef Claire said, pushing her coffee cup away. "He scared the hell out of me."

"I'm sure he did," Josie said.

"And I stayed scared for a couple of hours," she whispered as she stared off into the distance. "Then I got mad."

"What did you do?" I said, gripping the table with both hands.

"I waited," she said, shrugging. "I figured that he would eventually try to apologize or at least bring me something to eat. And when I heard the chain being removed, I hid behind the door. When he came into the room, he was carrying a tray with both hands, and I slugged him with my softball bat. Man, did I hit him hard."

"Nice to see that scholarship didn't go to waste," I said, managing a nervous chuckle.

"Hey, you don't make all-conference bunting," she said, laughing. "I caught him on the back of the head, and he went down like he'd been shot. Which he might have been if I'd had a gun. He was out cold, so I took the time to pack a bag, then I called 911 and left."

"Then you went to the cops, right?" Josie said.

"I certainly did. Tried to get him charged with kidnapping, but I had to settle for aggravated assault and felonious restraint. I don't know how his lawyer did it, but Charlie got off with probation again. But I did get a restraining order on him, which he tried to ignore a couple of times until one of the local cops I knew had a quiet word in his ear about what a good idea leaving L.A. might be. And then he left. And I didn't hear from him again until about six months ago."

"How did he find you?" Josie said.

"That was my own fault. The culinary school sent out this questionnaire asking alumni to update them on what we were doing. They were doing some big marketing campaign to attract new students and wanted to use some graduates' stories as part of it. I filled it out and didn't give it a second thought. Charlie saw it, then called me out of the blue one day."

"And told you he was only a hundred miles away," I said, shaking my head.

"Yeah, you can imagine how *delighted* I was to learn that," Chef Claire said, again drumming her fingers on the table.

"Why didn't you ever say anything to us?"

"I didn't want to worry you," she said, running her fingers through her hair. "Besides, what would you be able to do?"

"Oh, I can think of a lot of things I'd like to do to him," I said.

"You got that right," Josie said. "Do you think you're in danger?"

"No, I don't think Charlie would ever hurt *me*. But he's already shown that he's capable of going after other people he considers a threat," she said, shaking her head. "And I'm certainly not going to take that chance."

"We need to call the Chief," I said. "He'll help us get a new restraining order just in case he does show up."

Chef Claire thought about it, then nodded.

"Thanks for listening, guys," she said, managing a small smile. "I actually feel a bit better. So, how is Bobbie doing?"

"She's good," I said. "I like her."

"Me too," Josie said, nodding.

"Well, it's a good thing that she doesn't have to leave Ottawa. Charlie wouldn't like that at all."

"Yes, we noticed," I said. "He does seem overly protective."

"Charlie has a hard time distinguishing friends and family from possessions," Chef Claire said. "If you're in his life, he thinks you belong to him."

"But you, pardon the pun, knocked that belief out of him, right?" Josie said, grinning.

"So I thought."

Chapter 16

Deciding that the dog toy business and the prospect that Chef Claire's persistent and possibly dangerous ex-boyfriend might show up unannounced were more than enough to occupy my neurons, I pushed aside all the nagging questions about who might have killed Joshua Middleton and relegated them to my *I'll deal with that later* file.

I'd reread Bobbie's business plan several times and was still confused about why all of the banks she'd met with had turned her down. The pet service industry, of which dogs comprise the largest percentage, totals in the billions and is growing annually at a healthy clip. Sure, the dog toy business was a start-up, always a risky proposition for any lender, but the numbers and her strategy looked rock solid to me. And I'd seen other new companies get loans for ventures that didn't come close to the upside potential of Wags. But I was certainly no expert, and I wanted a second opinion, so I gave a copy of the business plan to the one person whose opinion I valued above all others when it came to making money.

But if you breathe a word to my mother I said that I'll vigorously deny it.

I was in my office handling some paperwork when she strolled in wearing a stylish winter coat over a sand-colored cashmere sweater and a pair of Horse-Hound tweed pants that fit like they'd been tailored specifically for her.

Which they probably were.

Regardless, she looked amazing and made me feel like a slob who'd fallen out of bed into a pair of old sweatpants and a wrinkled long-sleeved men's shirt that was four sizes too large.

Which I had.

She tossed the business plan on my desk, cast a disapproving glance at what I was wearing, then removed her coat and sat down on the couch. Chloe clamored out from under the desk and hopped up next to her.

"Can you believe it's starting to snow?" she said, shaking her head as she glanced out the window. "It's not even Thanksgiving."

"We'll be in the Caymans before you know it, Mom," I said, glancing out at the snowflakes drifting in the breeze. Instead of the sense of dread I felt most years at the onset of winter, I smiled as I watched the snow fall knowing that I'd be spending the worst winter months surrounded by white sand instead of mountainous snow banks. And ice and slush. And winds out of the north that took your breath away and froze your lungs if you weren't careful. I could almost feel the hot sun baking my body and a cold umbrella drink in my hand. I returned to the present and nodded at the business case. "What do you think?"

"I'm very surprised the banks weren't interested," she said, scratching Chloe's ears.

"So, it is good, right?"

"Yes, it's really good. And if you and the girls are looking for another partner, I suppose I could be coaxed into tagging along on this one," she said, giving me the crocodile smile she reserved for everyone who approached her with possible business opportunities.

"Would you be satisfied playing a completely passive role?"

"You know me better than that, darling," she said, laughing.

"Well, there's your answer," I said. "What would you do if you were me?"

"You have a couple of options," she said, draping one leg over the other. "You could just write a check and be done with it, but that's never a good way to go. Remember rule number one?"

"Always try to use other people's money," I said, nodding.

"Exactly. And since you'll be setting it up as a Canadian company, you should establish a solid relationship with at least one bank over there. You never know when it might come in handy."

"Yeah, that makes sense," I said, fiddling with my pen. "I thought that I might meet with one or two of the banks that already turned the loan down."

My mother gave me an odd smile.

"What is it?"

"I need to hear a bit more about why you'd meet with someone who has already said no," she said, her eyes dancing. "But I think I'm proud of you."

"You got a weird way of showing it," I said, shaking my head.

"Humor me."

"I want to see it for myself. I want to watch the expression on the banker's faces when they tell me no," I said. "And if any of them say yes, I want to know why the answer changed. Maybe they said no just because they weren't comfortable with Bobbie. Or maybe she said or did something they didn't like. And who knows, maybe they'll like the fact that we refused to take no for an answer."

"You're saying you just want to understand why," she said, smiling.

"Yeah, pretty much."

"Well done, darling."

"If you say so, Mom."

"I've always found the who, what, where and when to be the easy part," she said by way of explanation. "But getting to the why takes you to the core of most problems. That's where the motives live."

"The motives live in the why?"

"Yes, they do."

"You should put that on a tee shirt."

169

"*Why* would I do that, darling?" she said, raising an eyebrow.

"Funny, Mom," I said. "So, you think I should take another shot at the loan from a couple of the banks that already turned it down?"

"I do. But go alone. If they do have a problem with this woman, Bobbie, it might be hard for them to get to yes with her in the room. In fact, if you can handle telling a little white lie, you might want to infer that you've bought the rights to the idea from her and now have a controlling interest in the company. If you get a different answer than Bobbie did, that might tell you a lot."

"Interesting," I said, nodding. "I guess I can handle that."

"But under no circumstances do you let them know that you could easily write a check to fund it," she said. "If you want to get an honest reaction out of them, do your best to come across as a struggling entrepreneur who's just trying to catch a break. Wear your lumberjack outfit. That should do the trick."

"It's not a lumberjack outfit," I snapped. "It's jeans and a flannel shirt."

"Don't forget the boots," she said, shaking her head. "Seeing those things on your feet just breaks my heart."

"They're winter boots, and they're comfortable."

She glanced at her watch and stood up after gently sliding the sleeping Chloe off her lap.

"I'd love to stay and talk lumberjack fashion with you, darling, but I have a town council meeting to get to. Tonight is the night when I tell them, despite all their cajoling, I won't be running for reelection."

"Good for you, Mom," I said, knowing how much she hated being mayor, notwithstanding the fact that she was very good at it.

"I want to make sure I have as much free time as possible," she said, giving me a coy smile. "You know, just in case I'm ever fortunate enough to be blessed with a grandchild,"

Fastball right down the middle. I never got the bat off my shoulder.

"Yeah, Mom, I'll get right on that," I said, dismissing her with a gentle back of the hand wave.

"That would be wonderful, darling," she said on her way out of the office. "Just not in that dreadful lumberjack outfit. I only have so many years left."

I heard her laughing all the way to the front door.

Chapter 17

I entered the house through the kitchen door and was immediately steamrolled by my four best four-legged friends and a smell I was very familiar with. Josie was at the stove stirring a large pot and adding Cabernet to taste. She sampled the gravy, nodded her approval, then poured and handed me a glass of red wine.

"Beef stew?" I said, then took a sip.

"Yeah," Josie said, clinking glasses with me. "It's cold out, and I thought we were about due for some comfort food."

"Good call," I said, peering into the pot. "What are we having with it?"

"Cornbread."

"Perfect. You need a hand?"

"No, I got it. Chef Claire and the Chief are in the living room. Why don't you head in and take the beasts with you?" She glanced down and laughed when she saw Captain staring up at her with his head cocked. "Yes, I'm talking about you." She knelt down and gave him a big hug. The massive Newfie returned it and proceeded to knock Josie flat on her back on the kitchen floor.

"Good job, Captain," I said, laughing as I extended my hand to her. "Bobbie's not here yet?"

"No, I told her seven," Josie said, climbing to her feet and brushing herself off. She shook her head at Captain who seemed pleased with himself. "Goofball."

"Okay, we're out of here," I said, heading for the living room trailed by the four dogs. I gave Chef Claire and Chief Abrams a hug then sat down and fought for space with Captain and Chloe who apparently thought the couch had their name on it.

"We were just talking about the new restraining order," Chef Claire said. "The Chief said the judge signed it today."

"Hopefully, we won't need it," Chief Abrams said. "But it's good to have."

"He probably won't show up," Chef Claire said. "If he knows what's good for him."

"You got your bat?" I said, grinning at her.

"Oh, I've got my bat, don't worry."

We heard a soft knock on the kitchen door, and moments later Josie ushered Bobbie into the living room. She seemed tentative at first, but she and Chef Claire exchanged a warm hug. We introduced Bobbie to the Chief, got her a glass of wine, and she settled in next to massive Newfie who was staring at her intensely.

"Wow, you must be Captain," Bobbie said, rubbing the dog's head. "He's gorgeous. Actually, all four of them are. Who has the Goldens?"

"That would be me," Chef Claire said. "Meet Al and Dente."

Bobbie laughed at the names, then glanced around the room, and finally seemed to relax a bit.

"Were you able to get away…unnoticed?" Chef Claire said.

"Yeah," Bobbie said. "It's Charlie's day off, and he said something about going to a concert in Montreal."

"Okay," Chef Claire said, nodding. "So, how have you been?"

"Oh, I've had my ups and down," she said, managing a small smile. "But things seem to be looking up at the moment."

"Let's hope so," I said, noticing Josie carrying the pot of beef stew into the dining room.

"Dinner is served," Josie said, then herded the dogs to the kitchen door. "I think you guys can handle being outside for a while." She let the dogs out into the fenced area off the back of the house and closed the door behind them.

We sat down and ate quietly for a few minutes.

"This is really good, Josie," Chef Claire said, then turned to Bobbie. "I love your idea for the dog toys."

"Thanks, I hope we're able to get something off the ground," Bobbie said, glancing at me.

"Oh, we're going to do a lot more than just get off the ground," I said. "If you're happy with the 60/40 split, we're ready to go."

"I am," Bobbie said. "You should know that I would have agreed to 50/50."

"I know," I said, reaching for a slice of corn bread. "But that would have required us to do a whole lot more work." I laughed. "And we're about to head to the Caymans to open another restaurant and an animal shelter. But before we do, I plan on heading back up to Ottawa to meet with some of the banks that turned you down."

"Why would you do that?" Bobbie said, frowning.

"Mainly because I want to see the look in their eyes if they say no again," I said. "I'm still baffled about why they turned you down."

"Tell me about it," Bobbie said. "And it wasn't just the fact they said no, it was the way they did it. It was almost like they were reading from the same script."

"Really?" I said, frowning.

"Yeah, it was kinda weird. But then I figured bankers are all probably trained to say no the same way."

"Yeah, that's probably it," I said, glancing at Chef Claire, then at Josie.

"Uh-oh," Josie said, shaking her head. "She's got that look."

"She certainly does," Chef Claire said. "What's the matter?"

"Nothing," I said, shaking my head. "I'm just thinking."

"I knew I smelled something," Chief Abrams said, spooning another helping of beef stew onto his plate.

"Do you have the names of the banks you talked to?" I said to Bobbie.

"Sure. I'll never forget them, or the people who turned me down."

"Write them down for me before you go," I said, rubbing my forehead.

"What's on your mind, Suzy?" Chief Abrams said.

"I was just sitting here wondering if banks are susceptible to outside pressure," I said.

"I'm sure they can be at times," he said. "Where are you going with this? Some sort of conspiracy theory?"

I thought hard for a moment, then shook my head and focused on my dinner.

"Nah, that's just too goofy," I said, dismissing my own unspoken thought. Then I noticed Bobbie giving me a confused look. "What?"

"You just seemed to disappear for a second there," she said, shrugging.

"You'll get used to it," Chef Claire said.

"You'll even start looking forward to it," Josie deadpanned.

"Shut it."

Then we all sat upright when we heard the noise coming from outside the kitchen door. Then the dogs barked and transitioned into a chorus of guttural growls.

"I know that knock," Chef Claire said, setting her knife directly in front of her on the table. Then she turned to Bobbie. "I guess he changed his mind about Montreal."

"Chef Claire," Bobbie said. "I'm so sorry. He must have followed me."

"I assume you're talking about your brother?" Chief Abrams said, getting up from the table to peer through the window. "Around six feet, thin, blonde hair?"

"Yes, that's him," Chef Claire said. "I knew it."

"Well, the sooner we let him in, the sooner we can tell him to take a hike," Josie said.

"I'm going to stand over there out of the way," Chief Abrams said. "I want to see how he acts before he knows there's a cop in the room."

"I'll get the door," I said, getting up. I looked around the table, then at Chief Abrams who had taken up his position. "Are we ready?"

"Yeah, let's get this over with," Chef Claire said, her face drawn and drained of color.

I walked into the kitchen and opened the door.

"Charlie," I said, pleasantly. "What are you doing here?"

"I'm looking for my lying sister," he said, taking a step inside. "And Chef Claire. Is she here?"

"She's in the dining room," I said, blocking his path. "But let's not do anything crazy, okay?"

"I wouldn't think of it," he said, his eyes staring past me toward the dining room. "I just stopped by say hello."

"I'm not joking, Charlie," I said, glaring at him.

"Relax," he said. "Something smells good.

I took a step to one side, and he walked past me into the dining room. I followed and stood to one side as he glared at his sister, then beamed at Chef Claire.

"Hi," he whispered.

"Hello, Charlie," Chef Claire said evenly. "You shouldn't have come."

"That wasn't my plan," he said, his eyes glancing around the table. "But when my own sister has the audacity to lie to me, I always like to see what sort of mischief she's getting herself into."

Bobbie lowered her eyes and remained silent.

"It's nice seeing you, Charlie," Chef Claire said. "But it's time for you to leave."

"Leave? I just got here," he said, getting ready to sit down at the table.

"Don't make me get my bat, Charlie."

He flinched and took his hand off the chair.

"I thought we could talk, just the two of us. You know, catch up. It's been a long time."

"It's not gonna happen, Charlie," Chef Claire said, giving him a cold stare.

"Oh, I think we'll just have to see about that," he said, grinning at her.

"No, son, I don't think we will," Chief Abrams said, stepping into Charlie's line of sight.

"Who are you?" Charlie said.

"I'm Chief Abrams."

"A cop?" Charlie said, glancing back and forth between Chef Claire and Bobbie. "You called the cops?"

"Nobody called me," the Chief said. "I just happened to be here for dinner. And you need to leave."

"Says who?"

"Well, for starters, me, and this restraining order I have in my hand." Chief Abrams slipped the order into Charlie's hand. "You can keep that one. It's your copy."

Charlie scanned the document then tossed it on the table.

"Another restraining order? Chef Claire, how could you?" he said, his bottom lip quivering.

"Actually, Charlie, it wasn't that hard at all. You really need to leave."

"And if I don't?" he said, his breathing pattern now laboring.

"Then I'm going to arrest you for violating the order," the Chief said. "And any other charges you might give me a reason to slap on you."

"I can't believe this," Charlie said, clenching and unclenching his fists. "You sounded so friendly over the phone."

"No, I don't think I did, Charlie," Chef Claire said. "Please, go…and don't come back."

Charlie's eyes began to water, and he stared at her. Then he focused on his sister.

"You and I need to have a chat," he said, grabbing Bobbie's arm and jerking it hard.

"Ow," Bobbie said, determined not to be pulled from her chair. "Stop it, Charlie."

"Let go of her, son," Chief Abrams said evenly.

"Go away, old man. This is family business," Charlie said, glancing over his shoulder as he continued to pull Bobbie's arm.

"Okay, have it your way," the Chief said, shaking his head.

"That's right. My way," Charlie snapped as he strained to drag Bobbie out of her chair.

He was about to say something else but was stopped when the two electrodes from the taser Chief Abrams fired hit him in the lower back. He jerked and spasmed like he was dancing in a mosh pit then dropped onto the floor his body quivering. Chief Abrams left the electrodes right where they were until he had Charlie hands cuffed behind his back. He removed the electrodes then rolled him over. When Charlie was sitting on the floor with his back against a wall, Chief Abrams knelt down and leaned in close.

"You shouldn't have made that crack about my age, Charlie. And for the record, I'm not old, I'm just experienced."

Josie and I both snorted. Chef Claire and Bobbie continued to stare at the semi-conscious man with the blank expression on his face.

"Here's what we're going to do, Charlie," the Chief said, gently slapping his face to get his attention. "Stay with me here, Charlie. We're going to get you back in your car, and I'm going to follow you for a while until I'm sure you're on your way back to Ottawa. Just nod if you understand what I'm saying."

Charlie managed a small nod as he stared down at the floor.

"And then I'm going to make sure that all the cops in the area and all the customs and immigration agents on both sides of the border have your picture. If any of them see you heading anywhere near Clay Bay, they're gonna call me, Charlie. And the next time, I won't be using the taser on you. The next time I'm gonna ask Chef Claire if I can borrow her bat. Do you understand what I'm telling you, Charlie?"

Charlie nodded then Chief Abrams helped the wobbly man to his feet.

"Okay, I'm going to walk you out now. Then when I'm sure we truly understand each other, and your motor skills return, I'll take the cuffs off, and you'll be on your way. Got it?"

Charlie nodded and leaned against the wall breathing heavily.

"Now apologize for your behavior," the Chief said.

"What?"

"You heard me. Apologize."

"Sorry," Charlie whispered to the floor.

"Thanks for dinner, ladies. As always, there's never a dull moment around here," the Chief said, grabbing Charlie by the elbow. "We'll see ourselves out."

We watched as Chief Abrams led the still wobbly Charlie outside, then down the driveway. A few minutes later, two sets of headlights came on, and Charlie slowly drove off closely followed by the Chief.

"I'm so sorry," Bobbie said.

"Don't worry about it," Chef Claire said. "It's not your fault. And it had to happen eventually."

"Do you think he'll come back?" Bobbie said.

"No, I doubt it. Charlie's a lot of things, but he's not stupid," Chef Claire said. "Chief Abrams can be very persuasive. And he has a lot of friends."

"That's the first time I've ever seen anybody get tased," Bobbie said. "Nasty."

"It certainly was," I said.

"He got off easy," Chef Claire said, taking a bite of beef stew. "He's lucky I didn't get my bat."

Chapter 18

I crossed the border at Ogdensburg then headed for Ottawa in a downpour that was threatening to become freezing rain. As such, it turned my drive into a heart-pounding, white-knuckle journey along a sixty-mile stretch of slip and slide posing as Highway 416. Fortunately, traffic was light, and it appeared the only people on the road were truckers and idiots, like me, who didn't have enough sense to cancel their plans and stay home in front of the fire with a good book.

But the extra driving time gave my brain some quiet time to fully digest and reflect on what I'd discovered online while doing some digging into the life and times of Joshua Middleton. Convinced I had connected all the requisite dots, as soon as I got in my car I called the three banks I'd made appointments with. I canceled two, confirmed the third, then put my phone away after a deep puddle I hit doing forty produced a cascade of slush that scared me half to death when it thumped against my windshield. I cursed the relentless downpour of the dreaded *wintry mix*, prayed a temperature drop wouldn't force me to buy skates for the trip home, and soldiered on to my remaining appointment, fully convinced it would be the only one I'd need. What should have taken an hour, turned into two, and I was glad I'd left early because I barely managed to make it to my scheduled appointment on time.

I let the receptionist know I had arrived then headed to the bathroom to empty my nervous and very full bladder that had me tiptoeing across the Italian tile floor like a bow-legged chicken. I took a look in the mirror as I washed my hands, wasn't pleased by what I saw, then shrugged it off and tossed my bag over my shoulder and headed back out to the lobby. The receptionist got her first good look at what I was wearing. She blinked and gave me a sad smile, a combination of pity and surprise I had to acknowledge was probably warranted. She did everything she could to hide the smile on her face as she led me to an office, and I sat down and glanced around at the collection of photos on the desk and walls as I waited. I smiled and gave myself a mental pat on the back when my eyes settled on a series of photos on one of the walls.

Moments later, a man entered wearing a tailored dark blue suit paired with a crisp white shirt and a red tie emblazoned with a college insignia I didn't recognize. He glanced at my outfit, a peasant skirt and blouse combination my mother had laughingly dubbed colonial-schoolmarm, and beat back his frown with a small smile. He sat down across the desk from me and folded his hands in front of him.

"Ms. Chandler, right?" he said, giving me a smug, patronizing look.

"Yes, please, call me Suzy."

"Of course," he said, removing a fresh writing tablet from one of the desk drawers. "Suzy it is." He pulled his pen from his shirt pocket and clicked it several times, apparently to make sure it was still working, then carefully set it down on top of the tablet. Ready for battle, he folded his hands in front of him again and gave me the same smug look my subconscious was already urging me to knock into next week.

"And you're Wendell Powers?" I said, smiling as I reached into my bag and pulled out two copies of the business plan and set them down in front of me.

"I am," he said, fiddling with his pen again.

"Vice President of Commercial Lending?"

"*Senior* Vice President," he said, flashing a quick smile at my mistake. "I understand you'd like to borrow some money."

"Yes, I would," I said, sitting back in my chair.

We sized each other up. It wasn't hard to do. He was already figuring out a way to give me a polite but firm no in the shortest amount of time possible, while I was determined to confirm the reasons for his refusal, no matter how long it took. Fortunately, I'd come prepared for a lengthy battle. I reached into my bag and pulled out a fresh bag of Snickers.

"Bite-sized?" I said, holding out the bag to him.

"No, thanks," he said, tight-lipped as he glanced down at the loan application I'd filled out online. "Let's see, you'd like to borrow three million dollars."

I slid a copy of the business plan across the desk, and he stared down at it like it was cursed with a communicable disease.

"Actually, I only need two-point-nine-five, but if you want to round up, that would be fine with me."

"Of course," he said, then his tongue flickered like a lizard snatching a fly out of mid-air. "Let's see what we have here. Hmmm. Wags. A dog toy business, correct?"

"That's the one," I said, beaming at him as I popped one of the bite-sized and chewed.

"This is strange," he said, casually flipping through the document. "I just saw this exact business plan a few months ago."

"Really?" I said. "I did not know that."

"How is this possible?" he said, frowning at me.

"You know, I'm not really sure, Wendell," I said, getting a flinch out of him. Apparently, loan applicants didn't often have the temerity to call him by his first name. "I assume it's already made the rounds with various lending institutions. But I recently acquired the rights to the idea."

"I see. Good for you," he said, still frowning as he tried to wrap his head around why a loan application he'd already killed off had resurfaced.

"And I have a controlling interest in the company," I said, popping another bite-sized. "Are you sure you wouldn't like one of these?"

"No, I'm fine," he said, waving my offer off. "I'm afraid our bank has already turned this opportunity down. It was an interesting idea, but we decided to pass."

"You did?" It was my turn to frown. "Why on earth would you do that?"

He stared at me like I had questioned the identity of his birth mother.

"We had our reasons," he said, miffed at my having the audacity to ask the question.

"Yes, I'm sure you did. What were they?"

"Well, I'm sure that's really none of your concern," he said, emitting a sound that reminded me of gurgling water. "But you can rest assured, they were *very good* reasons."

"I see," I said, sliding the package of bite-sized back into my bag. "And none of the circumstances associated with those reasons have changed since you made your original decision?"

"No," he said softly. Then he gave me a puzzled look. "Why would you ask me that?"

"Oh, I just sort of put two and two together," I said, draping a leg over my knee. "I thought I got four, but maybe I was wrong."

"I'm really not following the thread of this conversation," he said, drawing indecipherable squiggles on his writing pad. "And if you'll excuse me for cutting our meeting short, I have another appointment to get to."

"I just thought that the recent vacancy on your board of directors might be enough to make you reconsider the original decision."

He gave me a wide-eyed stare then tossed his pen aside.

"What?"

"The vacancy on your board."

"Who are you?" he whispered.

"I'm Suzy. Suzy Chandler."

"Chandler?" he said, frowning. "Chandler. Where do I know that name from?"

"I have no idea," I said, knowing my lineage was about to be revealed.

"Don't tell me she's your mother?" he said, still staring at me.

"Yeah, she certainly is," I said, shrugging. "But she's not involved in this deal."

"Why didn't you say so?"

"Because it has nothing to do with her," I said. "This is all about why you turned down an opportunity like the one in front of you."

"I told you," he said, starting to backpedal. "We had our reasons."

"Well, now that Joshua Middleton is dead, I have to assume that those reasons have pretty much evaporated, right?"

He flinched and sat back in his chair. I'd blown the fastball right by him. It felt good, and I wondered what to throw next. I decided to lob one in so he could get a bit of his confidence back.

"Middleton was on your board, wasn't he?"

"Yes," he eventually managed to get out.

"Wow, that took a while," I said, grinning. "It sounded like a pretty easy question."

"Who sent you?"

"What?"

"Who put you up to this?"

"Put me up to what?" I said, feigning innocence. "I'm just a woman trying to secure a bank loan."

"Yeah, and I'm the Princess of Monaco." He sat back in his chair, draped a leg over his knee, and steepled his fingers against his chin. "Okay, what do you want to know?"

"I want to know why you and the rest of the people who run this place agreed to Middleton's demand."

"His demand?"

"Yes, his demand that you not fund this project," I said, pointing at the business plan. "It wouldn't be because he was going to steal the idea, wasn't he?"

"I have no idea what you're talking about," he said, shaking his head.

"It's okay, Wendell," I said, nodding. "I'm sure your bank wasn't unique. I imagine Middleton made the same demand to several other banks. He was on a lot of boards. Although it does appear that you and he had a very close working relationship."

"Mr. Middleton was a valued board member who will be sorely missed," he said, staring off into the distance at a photo of himself with Middleton on a golf course. They had their arms around each other's shoulder and were grinning at the camera like they owned the world. Which, I'm sure, was something on both of their bucket lists.

"Yeah, I saw that exact comment on the press release you guys put out after he got killed," I said, working my head back and forth until my neck popped. "Ah, that's better. Long car rides just kill me."

He stared at me, unsure where to take the conversation next. I decided to help him out.

"How much did Middleton plan on borrowing to get the dog toy business up and running?"

"What?" he said, dazed.

"I think three million is plenty, but I'm not a mogul like him. His *vision* was probably on a grander scale than mine. How big a loan did he want?" I said, hearing the irritation creeping into my voice. I couldn't tell if his reaction was a total act, or if this was, in fact, his normal behavior. Either way, he was really starting to annoy me.

Wendell tried to reclaim the higher ground, and he leaned forward and rested his elbows on the desk. "That's a very interesting theory, Ms. Chandler, but one that's highly offensive. And quite impossible to prove."

"Oh, I don't know, Wendell," I said, grinning at him as I pointed at the numerous photos of them on the wall. "The two of you were very good buddies and undoubtedly had a long track record of working together. He was on your board, and, as I was very surprised to learn, *you* were on *his*."

"To coin a phrase, Ms. Chandler, what does that have to do with the price of fish?"

"I don't know. I don't eat fish. But Middleton Enterprises is going through a rough patch, and he was dealing with a lot of anxious investors and shareholders. And then a world-class business idea gets laid on your desk. Just the sort of idea that Middleton had been asking you to keep an eye out for. We could spend all day debating it back and forth, but I imagine it would be easier just to find somebody with *oversight* responsibilities to do a little digging into your loan files. I'm pretty sure any investigator worth her salts could come up with all sorts of relevant information about your prior...*transgressions*." I paused to take a breath and flash him my best smile. "The people I've been talking to are saying I'm thinking way too far out of the box on this one. What do you think?"

"I think you're out of your mind."

"Tomato, tomahto," I said with a shrug.

"It's a ridiculous suggestion," he said, deciding to try pouting.

"But the dog toy line is an amazing idea that fits perfectly into Middleton's business model. And it certainly has a lot more potential for growth than pet massage salons, wouldn't you say?"

He stared at me like Chef Claire had just tattooed him between the eyes with her bat.

"Pet massage?" he whispered.

"Yeah, I believe the name of the woman who came up with that idea is Wilma Firestone. Let me ask you a question, did you and Middleton only try to steal business ideas from female entrepreneurs, or were you guys gender-neutral?"

"I'm going to ignore that comment," he said, going for wounded pride, but coming up short.

"You know, I'm still not sure if you were the one who brought the pet massage idea to Middleton, or if he just happened to stumble onto it when Wilma was doing the *laying of hands* thing on him. But it shouldn't be hard to confirm it with her. Or with Victor Rollins for that matter."

"Victor Rollins?" Wendell said, raising an eyebrow at me. "What does he have to do with any of this?"

"From what I saw the other day, I think he and Wilma are getting pretty tight," I said, then decided to go with another white lie I was sure my mother would approve of. "And Victor and I go way back."

Wendell had apparently run out of ways to fend me off because he spread his arms wide and stared across the desk.

"Okay, what do you want, Ms. Chandler?"

192

"I want a business loan for three million bucks," I said, shrugging. "And I also want to find out who killed Middleton."

"I'm sure we can take another look at the loan," he said softly. "But I have no idea who killed Joshua."

"I'm sure you don't," I said, shrugging at him as I stood up. "I'll be going now, Wendell. Thanks for your time. Can I assume I'll be hearing from you soon?"

"Yes, you will," Wendell said, getting up and extending his hand. "Our loan committee is meeting tomorrow. I will personally give you a call as soon as I get a decision."

"And that decision will be a yes, right?" I said, returning the handshake.

"I'd be very surprised if it wasn't, Ms. Chandler."

"Oh, call me, Suzy. Thank you, Wendell," I said, beaming at him. "I'm looking forward to doing business with you."

"You'll excuse me if I tell you that I'm less than thrilled about that prospect at the moment," he said flatly.

"Don't worry, Wendell," I said, waving as I headed toward the door. "I'm sure I'll grow on you."

"Yeah, like a fungus," I heard him whisper on my way out of the office.

But I was too keyed up to worry about the cheap shot at the moment. My neurons were firing on all cylinders, and I headed for my car through the torrential pounding of rain and snow that was turning the pavement into a pile of cold slush. Satisfied that it still wasn't officially freezing rain, I climbed into the driver seat and pulled my phone out of my pocket.

"Fungus, huh?" I said as I waited for the call to connect. "Well played, Wendell."

Chapter 19

"Ms. Chandler," an irritated Victor Rollins said into the phone. "My assistant said you needed to speak to me about an urgent matter. What can I do for you?"

"Hey, Victor," I said cheerfully as I gripped the steering wheel with both hands. "Can you hear me all right?"

"Unfortunately, yes," Rollins said.

"Oh, don't be like that, Victor. You wouldn't believe how hard it's raining in Ottawa," I said, inching around a stalled truck that was parked on the side of the road. "I think Mother Nature woke up on the wrong side of the bed this morning."

"Actually, I'm looking out the window at the moment. It's not freezing yet, right?"

"No, it's not," I said, then frowned. "You're still in Ottawa?"

"Yes, the police requested that I stick around for a while, remember?" he said, sounding tentative.

"Yeah, but they removed that restriction several days ago," I said, remembering the conversation I'd had with Bill and Shirley at lunch. Then a neuron fired and I smiled. "I hope Wilma is doing well."

"What?"

"Wilma. How's she doing?"

"Uh, I'm sure she's doing fine. Again, how can I help you?"

"I have a couple of questions I was hoping you'd be able to answer," I said, giving up my battle with the rain and pulling into a grocery store parking lot. I left the engine running but turned the wipers off to give them a much-needed rest. "I just came from a meeting with Wendell Powers."

"You have my deepest sympathies," he said, sounding sincere.

"So, you do know Wendell?"

"Of course. He's a member of our board of directors."

"And a close personal friend of Middleton, right?"

"Well, he *was*."

"Sure, sure."

"Can I ask why you were meeting with him?"

"I needed a business loan," I said.

"You should know that the man's a total shark," Rollins said, then chatted briefly with someone on his end of the phone.

"Is that Wilma?" I said, grinning.

"Yes," he whispered. "If you must know, as a matter of fact, it is."

"Tell her I said hi. Yeah, I figured out that Wendell is definitely someone to keep an eye on. But I think I'll be able to keep him under control."

"You'll have to share your secret with me. Look, I'm right in the middle of a most enjoyable afternoon. Is there a point to this conversation?"

"Actually, there is," I said, grimacing as the rain pounded down even harder. "Have the police talked to you lately?"

"Just yesterday," he said. "Although they have absolutely no proof, apparently, I'm still suspect number one."

"Not for much longer, Victor. You're about to be completely cleared."

"Is that right?" he said, finding my comment very funny for some reason.

I waited out the laughter then continued.

"Yes, I think I can help you with that. But I need you to answer a question first."

"Your willingness to help me get off the list of suspects is dependent on how I answer a question?"

"Oh, no," I said, frowning. "You're going to get off that list regardless of how you answer. You didn't kill him. What is dependent on how you answer the question is whether or not I'm going to do whatever I can to help you get the CEO slot at Middleton Enterprises."

I could tell that he hadn't been expecting the curveball I'd just thrown, and I was forced to wait out a lengthy silence.

"So, in addition to being a dog devotee, now you're adding people to the mix?"

"Funny, Victor."

"You must be quite the miracle worker. You really believe you can help me get the job?"

"I'm not sure," I said, studying the torrent of water streaming off my windshield. Still, no signs of freezing. "But I think I can do a few things that might help."

"Like what?"

I heard the sound of ice cubes rattling.

"You know, Victor. That's an annoying habit."

"What on earth are you talking about?"

"Rattling your ice cubes," I said. "And isn't it a bit early in the day to be getting into the scotch?"

"Who are you, my mother?" he snapped. "Not that it's any of your business, but I'm on vacation, and I'm certainly not going anywhere in this weather. Only idiots are out on the road today."

Fastball right down the middle I never saw coming.

"Fair point," I said, nodding. "Okay, here comes my question."

"I can't wait."

"What do you know about Middleton's plans to get into the dog toy business?"

I stared at my phone as I waited out another long silence.

"Dog toys? I have no idea what you're talking about," he said flatly.

I decided to believe him for the moment.

"He never said anything about stealing the idea from someone else and then setting it up as part of Middleton Enterprises?"

"No, he didn't," Rollins said, rattling his ice cubes. "But that's not surprising. Ever since I first confronted him about stealing other people's ideas, Joshua stopped confiding in me about that particularly offensive *business strategy*. His term, not mine."

"So, you were aware he wasn't above doing that?"

"Above doing it?" Rollins said, laughing. "Middleton had an active outreach effort in place. He and Wendell were always on the lookout for the next great idea to steal."

"And you confronted him about it?"

"For a while," he said softly. "That was the reason why he was doing everything he could to shove me to the side. I'd stopped trying to talk to him about it, but it turns out that I'd asked a few more times than he was comfortable with."

"I thought you were being hung out to dry because some of the regions you're responsible for were tanking," I said, trying to remember the details of what Chief Abram's buddy had conveyed to him.

"I have no idea where you got that tidbit, but you seem to be full of surprises. For the record, they were *tanking* because Joshua was constantly sticking his nose where it didn't belong. One day he'd be telling all of the franchise owners to do something stupid, the next it would be a completely different directive. Usually, something even dumber."

"Just to make you look bad and take you out of the picture?" I said, popping one of the bite-sized.

"That was part of it," he said. "He was worried that I might start chatting with the wrong people about what he was doing. And he definitely had a plan to take me out. But mostly, Josh was losing his grip. And when CEO's start losing it, one of the things they usually aren't shy about doing is taking out other people they see as a threat. You know, eliminate any and all logical successors to the throne."

"Sure, sure. Like on Game of Thrones, right?"

"Well, in Josh's case, it was more like Caligula," Rollins said. "But he had Wendell on the board to handle the politics, and as long as the stock didn't fall off a cliff, he was pretty much untouchable. And if he hadn't been killed, I probably would have been gone in a couple of months."

"Fascinating," I said, then corrected myself. "Actually, I'll go as far as interesting."

He laughed into the phone. Then I heard the sound of liquid being poured over ice. I heard him swallow, then he rattled his ice and cleared his throat.

"You punched him in the ballroom because of what he did to Wilma, didn't you?"

"It was certainly on my list of reasons. It was a disgusting thing to do."

"Yes, it was. But she kinda set herself up for it, right?"

"Maybe," he said, after a long pause.

"She's sitting right next to you, isn't she?" I said, chuckling.

"Yup," he said, laughing.

"Okay, new topic."

"Let's talk about how you think you can help me get the CEO job. Not that I think you can."

"Oh, I just thought that if you were able to bring a new deal to the table, potentially a very big deal, that might help your chances."

"I suppose it could," Rollins said. "Our revenue model is pretty static, and we're getting close to being maxed out on new franchise locations."

"How many franchises do you guys have?"

"Just under fifteen hundred."

"Wow. I like that number a lot," I said, my neurons colliding all over the place.

"I have no idea why it would make any difference to you," he said. "But why do I feel like you're about to drop something on me?"

"Oh, I am, Victor," I said, breathing a sigh of relief as the rain finally began to soften. "What would you say to the exclusive, North American distribution rights to a new product line that has the potential to be the biggest thing since Beanie Babies?"

"Beanie Babies? Now there's a blast from the past," he said. "I used to collect them when I was a kid."

"A lot of us did," I said. "And we think the idea is ripe for a comeback. But with a dog twist."

"You lost me."

"You remember my question about the dog toys?"

"The idea that Middleton was trying to steal?" Rollins said.

"Yeah. But I'm sure Wendell was also involved."

"Then it must be a good one," he said. I heard the sound of his glass being set down on a wood surface. I assumed that was his signal I had his undivided attention. "What's your involvement with this thing?"

"It's a startup, and I'm one of the owners. But don't worry, Victor, my role will be more of a silent partner."

"I'll believe that when I see it."

"Funny," I said, then turned serious. "And trust me on this one, Victor. We won't be losing a hundred grand a year on it."

"All right, go ahead and give me the short version."

I spent the next five minutes outlining the basics of Bobbie's idea. He asked a few clarification questions, but mostly let me prattle on without interruption. When I finished, I sat back in my seat and waited out another long silence.

"I like it," he said, eventually. "Have you considered offering the toys as part of an online subscription service?"

"We have," I said. "And we've decided to keep that side of the business in-house and run it ourselves. But the only other

202

place people will be able to find the toys would be at your stores."

"You got a business plan?"

"We've got everything in place."

"Copyrights, patents?"

"I just said we have everything in place."

"Okay, there's no need to get snarky."

"And there's no need for you to assume we don't know what we're doing."

"Got it," he said softly. "I apologize. Why are you bringing this deal to me?"

"A couple of reasons. You're the biggest player in the industry, and we always like to deal with the fewest number of business partners possible. We've found that it makes everyone's life a lot simpler. And because you've got an incredible market footprint, you can move a lot of product in a hurry."

"Yes, we're very good at that when we get behind something," he said.

"I also thought that since you're a known entity to us, and we have some semblance of a relationship, strained as it is, bringing the deal to you might shorten our time to market. You know, avoid all that wining and dining crap."

He laughed.

"Wining and dining crap?"

"You know what I mean."

"Yes, I do. I'm very familiar with it."

"And as soon as I started putting together some of the things that Middleton was up to, I actually started to feel a bit sorry for you."

"You're joking, right?"

"No, it's true. You're a total pain in the neck, but you seem to be somebody who's overdue to catch a break. And if we're able to help you get the job, that has to help our position, right? I'm not sure it would give us any real leverage, but my guess is that it would provide us with a bit of *leeway* with you should we ever need it."

"Interesting take. Is there anything else?"

"There's just one more thing," I said. "I thought you'd appreciate the rather *ironic symmetry* associated with the deal."

"Ironic symmetry," he said, chuckling as he rattled his ice cubes. "Can I ask you a question?"

"Sure."

"What's it like living with your brain?"

"It's sort of like having family members as houseguests who don't know when it's time to leave," I said, laughing. "The past couple of days have been pretty chaotic inside my head."

"Did you put this together by yourself?"

"No, I had lots of help," I said, deflecting. "And the business plan came from our CEO."

"I'd like to meet him."

"Her."

"Oh. Sorry for the assumption," he said, quietly. "Look, it's a great idea, but I'm not sure Wendell is going to warm up to it. And he certainly wouldn't agree to anything that might help me get the CEO slot. Our relationship is pretty strained, and he's got a lot of juice with the board."

"You should give him a call," I said. "I think you might find him quite amenable to the idea."

"Why is that?"

"Because he's about to loan us three million bucks to get the thing off the ground," I said, grinning at myself in the rearview mirror.

"You got three million out of Wendell? Well done."

"At first, he didn't like the idea very much. And then we had a little chat about some of the things he and Middleton were up to."

"Playing a little hardball again, huh?" he said, laughing. "I'll need to watch my step around you."

"Ah, don't worry about that," I said. "You'll barely know I'm there."

"Again, I'll believe that when I see it."

"I need to run, Victor. The rain has stopped, and I still have a couple of things to take care of. I'm going to have Bobbie, our CEO, get in touch with you. And in the meantime, you should give Wendell a call."

"I'll do that," he said, giving his ice cubes one final rattle close to the phone.

"You did that just for my benefit, didn't you?"

"Oh, you caught that?" he said, laughing. "I'm glad you called, Suzy. This day has definitely taken a very weird turn for the better."

"Weird's the word for it. Later, Victor."

I ended the call and immediately placed another. As I waited for it to connect, I turned my wipers on to clear away the final remnants of the deluge. There was still no sign of the sun, but the temperature was holding steady. The fact that it looked like I'd be able to drive home later without having to worry about ice-covered roads was consoling, but my mood still turned sullen as I realized that the fun part of my day was officially over.

"Detective Billet speaking," said the voice on the other end of the line.

"Hi, Shirley. It's Suzy Chandler. You got a minute to chat?"

Chapter 20

Bill and Shirley, the lovebird cops who'd been assigned the Middleton investigation, a politically-sensitive and media-friendly murder case that was undoubtedly putting a serious dent in their alone time, reluctantly agreed to leave the warm, dry comfort of the police station only after I was able to convince them that the Slushie-storm had stopped. My offer to buy them a late lunch sealed the deal, and I pulled into the parking lot of an Italian restaurant they'd suggested not far from where they worked. They were already sitting next to each other at a table set for four when I arrived. I greeted them with a small wave and sat down across from them. I glanced back and forth and frowned when I noticed their stares.

"What? Do I have chocolate on me?" I said, looking down and wiping my mouth with a napkin.

"What on earth are you wearing?" Shirley said, squinting at my ensemble.

"Oh, that," I said, waving it off. "I purposely dressed down for my appointment this morning."

"I certainly hope so," she said, shaking her head.

"Yeah, it's pretty bad," I said, reaching for a menu. "My mother called it colonial-schoolmarm."

"She was being kind," Bill said, laughing. "It's more like early Russian peasant. Did your strategy work? You know, the dressing down part."

"Like a charm," I said. "He hated me at first sight. It was beautiful."

Our waitress arrived to take our orders. I went along with their suggestion to have the baked ziti, and I sat back and relaxed for the first time in hours. Now that the business portion of my day was over, I felt the familiar tingle of adrenaline begin to work its way through my system.

"Over the phone, you said something about Middleton stealing business ideas," Shirley said.

"Yeah, it was a despicable business practice," I said. "And the banker he was partnered with is up to his neck in it."

"And you want us to arrest him?" Bill said, frowning.

"No way," I said, shaking my head. "I want Wendell right where he is for the moment. Other people will sort him out in due time."

"He didn't have anything to do with Middleton's murder?" Shirley said.

"No, I'm sure he didn't," I said, leaning forward and going for sage-cop. "The guy is a major white-collar scumbucket who should have been deep-sixed a long time ago, but any connection between him and whoever dirt-napped Middleton would have to be considered tangential."

They were both taking a drink of water but paused mid-sip. Like a pair of synchronized swimmers, they set their glasses down, blinked at me, then sat back in their chairs and stared across the table.

"Sorry," I said, giving them an embarrassed tight-lipped smile as I beat back a rush of adrenaline. "Bad habit. I was binge watching old cop shows last night.

"Okay, Kojak, as much as we appreciate your fluency in TV-cop, I think we're probably going to need a bit more," Bill said, leaning forward and placing his elbows on the table.

I launched into a lengthy overview of what Middleton and Wendell had been up to then told them about our plans for the dog toy company. When I finished, they seemed entertained by my story but confused about how it connected to their open murder case.

"While we're delighted to get a free lunch, Suzy," Shirley said. "I'm not sure I understand why you were so insistent we get together."

"That's where the tangential part comes in," I said, grinning.

"Well, thanks for clearing that up," Shirley said, glancing over at Bill.

They were holding hands between their plates, and I noticed the wedding ring was now gone from Bill's hand. I decided not to pry, considered it a sign of personal growth, and turned my attention to the warm Italian bread the waitress had placed in front of us. I grabbed a piece, dredged it in olive oil, and beamed as I chewed.

"Good, huh?" Bill said, reaching for the bread basket and offering it to Shirley.

"Amazing," I said, trying to wait patiently for Shirley to remove her hand from the basket before I went back for a second piece. "Did you bring the case file?"

"I did," Bill said, reaching into his bag and sliding the thick file across the table. "What do you expect to find in there?"

"I have a nagging thought that is driving me crazy," I said, opening the file.

"Only one?" Bill said, laughing. "Consider yourself lucky."

I flipped through the section that contained all the fingerprints they'd collected. I located mine, glanced at my thumb, and compared it with the black swirls on the page. I frowned and looked at my thumb again.

"What's the matter?" Bill said.

"Nothing," I said, shaking my head. "It's just that I've never seen my fingerprints before. It's hard to believe they're all unique."

"If they weren't, our jobs would be a whole lot harder," Shirley said.

"You got that right," Bill said. "Unless we weren't worried about arresting the right guy."

They both laughed hard. Cop humor, I decided, then laughed along with them. I continued to flip through the thick section that contained all the fingerprints.

"Still nothing on the prints, huh?" I said.

"No," Bill said, shaking his head. "Just Middleton's on the can of drain cleaner."

"And you got everyone's who was around that night?"

"If we missed anybody, I have no idea who they are," Shirley said.

"You got all the serving staff who were working that night?" I said, raising an eyebrow.

"Yup," Bill said, bored with my line of questioning.

"All the kitchen staff?"

"Yup."

"And did anything come back when you ran the prints through the computer?" I said, mindlessly flipping through the pages.

"Sure, lots of stuff," Shirley said. "You can't run five hundred sets of prints through the system and not get any hits. But it was all small stuff. Nothing that would raise a red-flag in this case."

I nodded and flipped to another section of the file. This one contained all the crime scene photos, and I grimaced when I saw Middleton on his back in the storage room with foam streaming out of his mouth. I turned the page, then slid the file to one side when the waitress approached with our meals. I grabbed my fork and took a bite of the steaming ziti, then nodded, impressed, and searched for a chunk of Italian sausage. As I ate, Bill and Shirley chatted quietly as I slowly flipped through the photos. I landed on a wide shot of the storage room, was about to turn the page, but stopped and stared at it. I put my fork down and held the file with both hands as I studied the photo.

"Are you having a stroke?" Bill said, genuinely concerned as he placed a hand on my forearm.

"No, I'm fine," I said, although I wasn't sure. I rubbed my forehead and continued to bore a hole in the photo as I concentrated hard. But nothing coalesced, and I eventually sat back and picked up my fork.

"What on earth is the matter with you?" Shirley said, leaning forward to take an upside-down look at the photo.

"I'm not sure," I said, scowling. "But I think I'm having some sort of déjà vu. Something about this photo is very familiar."

"You're probably just flashing back to the original scene," Bill said. "It happens sometimes. Seeing something that gruesome creates intense memories. Almost like it's been imprinted inside your head."

"Yeah, I've got lots of those imprints," I said, glancing over at him. "But that's not it. What on earth is it about this photo that looks so familiar?"

I slid my plate of half-eaten ziti away and glanced down at the photo again. I placed my elbows on the table, lowered my head and closed my eyes as I rubbed my temples.

"C'mon, fire," I whispered.

"Are you talking to us?" Shirley said.

"Probably not a request she should make to a couple of cops."

They shared another long laugh. I waited it out.

"No, I'm talking to my neurons," I said, not looking up. I continued to massage my temples as I concentrated. "C'mon, you can do it. It's right there. C'mon."

Then I sat upright in my chair and stared off into the distance. The lovebird cops looked at me like I'd lost my mind. I took another look at the wide shot of the storage room and traced the photo with my finger.

"I can't believe it. That's how he did it," I said, nodding to myself. "Unbelievable."

"Talk to us, Suzy," Bill said, glancing at Shirley.

"What do you see?" she said.

"The stamped tin ceiling," I said, pointing at the photo.

"That stuff is all over the hotel," Bill said, reaching for the file and studying the photo. "They call it part of their historical charm or some crap like that."

"Yes, it is," I said. "It's everywhere. But not that pattern. There's only one other place on the main floor where I've seen the same pattern." I stared off into the distance again and asked myself a question. "Can it be that simple?"

"Do you have any idea what she's talking about?" Bill said to Shirley.

"Not a clue," she said, shrugging.

"We need to head over to the Chateau Lavalier," I said, closing the file and reaching for my plate.

"Now?" Bill said, preparing to stand up.

"No, after we finish eating," I said, digging back into my ziti. "Relax, there's no hurry."

Bill stared at me, baffled. He looked at Shirley.

"You know who she reminds me of?"

"I was just sitting here thinking the same thing," Shirley said. "Officer Fredericks, right?"

"Exactly," Bill said.

"Who's Officer Fredericks?" I said.

"She used to be our office *visionary*," Shirley said. "She was always getting what she called vibrations from case files."

"Sounds like an interesting woman," I said, reaching for another piece of bread. "Is she still around?"

"No, she went away a few years ago," Bill said.

"Transferred?"

"No, institutionalized," he said, giving me a small smile. "Apparently, she's okay most days as long as she gets her meds."

"And is handcuffed to the bed," Shirley said.

"One too many vibrations?" I said, dredging the bread in olive oil.

"She got the idea in her head that our police chief was a serial killer," Shirley said. "It didn't end well for her."

"Well, don't worry about me," I said, spearing a piece of sausage. "I won't be making any false accusations. I know exactly who killed Middleton."

"Do you plan on letting us in on your little secret?" Shirley said, laughing.

"Of course, right after lunch," I said, then caught a glimpse of the cart our waitress was pushing toward our table. "Okay, who's up for dessert?"

Chapter 21

I followed them to the Chateau Lavalier in my car and was greeted by the same young man who'd been working the day Josie and I arrived for the conference. He opened the door, flinched at my outfit, then recovered and was about to welcome me to the hotel when he recognized me. He beamed at me and extended a hand to help me out of the car.

"Welcome back," he said. "Is there a costume party going on here tonight I don't know about?"

"You really need to consider a career in stand-up," I said, making a face at him.

"Actually, that's what I do," he said, shrugging. "And as soon as I start making more than twenty bucks a night doing it, I'm so out of here." He smiled at me as he gave my outfit another look. "Tragic," he said, shaking his head.

"Please leave it out front," I snapped, stepping away from the car. "I'm just here for a…meeting."

"Will do," he said, hopping in behind the wheel. "Simply tragic."

I heard him laughing as he drove off and I joined Bill and Shirley then followed them into the hotel. They headed straight for the manager's office, an old friend by now I assumed, and he listened to them explain why we were there. He checked his computer screen then confirmed that the ballroom was empty. The head of hotel security arrived, and he escorted us down the hallway and into the massive room where a handful of staff were setting up for a function. The security head excused himself, and we walked across the ballroom until we reached the storage room where Middleton had died.

We stepped inside and closed the door behind us. Bill set the case file on a stack of boxes and opened it to the page that contained the photo. He removed it from its plastic holder and held it out in front of him. I leaned over his shoulder and pointed at the markings that had caught my attention in the restaurant. We glanced up and identified the section that appeared slightly different from the rest of the stamped tin ceiling.

"Yeah, I get it," he said, frowning. "But I'm still not sure what it means."

"Look at the discoloration," I said, pointing up. "It's a square."

"You think it drops down?" Shirley said.

"I think it might," I said. "Did you guys ever check it out?"

Bill and Shirley shook their heads at each other.

"No, to be honest," he said. "I'm pretty sure I looked up and just took it for what it is. An antique stamped tin ceiling."

"Me too. This place has to be over a hundred years old. Things like that ceiling are bound to age differently in some places, right?" Shirley said, glancing at Bill for confirmation.

I hadn't meant to question their abilities, but they both seemed mildly annoyed with me. Then I caught the looks they were giving each other and realized they were more likely mad at themselves for having missed it the first time around. Shirley grabbed a step ladder that was leaning against a wall. She carried it across the room and set it up directly underneath the discolored section.

"It's such a minor difference, who would have even thought to give it a second look?" Bill said, staring up.

"Not me," I said, stepping back to give him room to climb the ladder.

He reached the ceiling and examined the patterned tin closely.

"I can see what looks like a faint outline of a square that's been cut into the ceiling, but it fits together like a glove. And there's no handle or anything else you could use to lower it." He began fiddling with one of the raised sections of the patterned tin.

"Well, how about that."

He glanced down at us, then refocused on the ceiling and slid one of the raised pieces to one side to reveal a small latch. He pulled the latch, and a four-foot square of the ceiling opened at a forty-five-degree angle. A folding ladder emerged. Shirley reached up and pulled it down until the steps touched the floor. Bill climbed down the ladder, then headed up the other. Halfway up he paused to remove a large flashlight that was clipped to his

218

belt then continued his climb. He reached the top of the ladder, stepped through the opening, and briefly disappeared from view. For a few seconds the only thing we could see was the beam of the flashlight, then the overhead space was flooded with light.

"It's another storage space," he called down. "C'mon up."

Shirley and I climbed the ladder and stepped into a big space we could easily stand up in. It contained stacks of boxes filled with a wide variety of cleaning and food-related supplies.

"Okay, I get it," Bill said, putting his hands on his hips as he looked around. "The murderer was hiding up here, climbed down to take Middleton out, then came back up here and closed the ladder behind him. And after everybody, including us, cleared out later that night, he just climbed down and walked out. It's perfect."

"I think he definitely came down through this opening to kill him," I said. "But he didn't hang around after he did it. He left straight away."

"No, I don't think so," Shirley said. "That would have been too risky. There were several hundred people within fifty feet of here."

"I agree," Bill said. "Much too risky. It would have been much safer just to sit up here and wait it out."

"No," I said, shaking my head. "He couldn't do that. His absence would have been noticed."

Bill sat down on a short stack of boxes and folded his arms across his chest.

"Talk to me, Suzy," he said softly.

"It would have been noticed because he was working that night," I said. "And he didn't leave through that opening. He used a different one."

Bill and Shirley glanced around the storage space then back at me, waiting for clarification.

"C'mon," I said. "Follow me. I think I've got this figured out."

I veered right and began to wind my way through the stacks. The path was narrow but well-defined. After we'd gone about thirty feet, I stopped when I noticed a piece of elaborate grillwork along the far wall that sat behind some ventilation ducts. I held my finger to my lips to request silence then knelt down and peered through the opening that looked down into the kitchen. Bill and Shirley knelt beside me, and we stared down at the flurry of noisy activities taking place about fifteen feet below.

"Your theory is that one of the kitchen staff killed Middleton?" Shirley whispered.

"Yeah," I said, focusing on Charlie who was working his hands through a big bowl filled with a wet sticky substance. Then I pointed. "Him."

"The guy in the chef's hat?" Bill whispered.

"Yeah," I said, dealing with a mixture of sadness and elation. "That's him. Chef Charlie."

"And he's wearing rubber gloves," Shirley said.

"He's mixing his secret sauce that goes in the corn fritter batter. The chili he uses is so hot, it can burn your skin," I whispered.

"And people still eat these things?" Shirley said. "I love spicy food, but that sounds a bit over the top."

"They're delicious," I said. "They definitely get your attention, but it's a *flavorful* heat. I think he cuts the intensity of the chili with mint and yogurt."

"Interesting."

Bill gently cleared his throat to get our attention.

"Sorry," I said, embarrassed.

We watched for a few moments then got to our feet and took a few steps back from the opening.

"The chef killed Middleton?" Shirley said, frowning.

"Yeah," I said softly. "I'm afraid so."

"That's almost as bad as saying the butler did it," Bill said, giving me a scowl. "If he was working that night, how the heck did he manage to pull off that miracle?"

"Follow me," I said, continuing down the narrow pathway.

After we slowly inched our way forward about another fifty feet, I came to a stop and pointed at an opening that was identical to the one above the storage room. Light streamed up from the floor below, and we caught a glimpse of the ladder that extended down to the break room. We heard a thump and hung back in the shadows. The thump was followed by the sound of a man whistling and humming a melody I didn't recognize.

"Hey, I know that tune," Shirley said. "It's a Russian folk song my mother used to sing to me."

"You're Russian?" I said, surprised.

"First generation," she said, beaming with pride.

We slowly made our way out of the shadows and the man, holding an industrial-sized can of tomato sauce under each arm, stopped humming when he saw us. Apparently, two uniformed cops and a woman who was dressed like one of his Russian peasant aunts was the last thing he expected to see while restocking. He dropped both cans of sauce and gave us an open-mouthed, wide-eyed stare that would have made Marty Feldman proud. Then he wheeled around and made a dash for the ladder screaming at the top of his lungs.

"Immigratsiya! Bezhat' za kholmami!"

"What did he say?" I said, frowning.

"Immigration," Shirley said. "Run for the hills."

"Rasslab'tes'. My ne immigratsiya," Shirley called after the man who had reached the top step.

I'm pretty sure Shirley had told the man we weren't from immigration, but either he didn't hear it or simply chose not to believe her. He glanced back over his shoulder at us as he started his descent down the ladder, missed a step, then bounced and tumbled until he landed face-first on the floor. We raced to the opening and stared down at the semi-conscious kitchen worker. He shook the fall off, glanced back up at us, then climbed to his feet and scrambled out of the break room. I had to admire the guy's toughness: That fall would have put me out of commission for at least a week.

"Immigratsiya! Bezhat' za kholmami! Bezhat' za kholmami! Yebat' menya."

"He added something at the end," I said, glancing at Shirley. "What did he say?"

"I'm not comfortable using that kind of language," she said, shaking her head.

We made our way down the ladder and stood in the doorway of the break room looking on. Several staff members were hurriedly collecting their things and heading out the back door. Chef Charlie, holding a very large kitchen knife, was walking toward us, thoroughly confused by the commotion.

"Where the heck are you guys going?" he said to no one in particular.

"Immigratsiya," one of the workers blurted as she ran past him out the door.

"Immigration?" Charlie said, frowning. Then he saw us standing in the doorway. "Suzy? What on earth are you doing here?"

"Oh, we just thought we'd pop in," I said casually as I glanced around at the rapidly emptying kitchen. "Got a sec?"

Charlie continued to stare at me then he tossed the knife he was holding onto a nearby butcher block and shrugged. "Sure," he said. "It's not like I'm going to be getting a lot of orders out for a while." He gestured at the break room and headed in and took a seat.

We sat down at the table next to him. Bill took the seat closest to the door, a move on his part I'm sure was strategic.

"Oh, how rude of me," I said. "This is Shirley. And that's Bill."

"I remember them," Charlie said, nodding at them. "Officers."

"Of course, you've already met," I said. "Duh."

"Well, I know you're not moonlighting for Canadian Immigration," Charlie said, drumming the table with his fingers. "Why are you here?"

I noticed several fresh bandages on his fingers and hands. Even though he definitely seemed to be a klutz with a knife, I was glad he'd left behind the big one he'd been holding in the kitchen. I glanced back and forth at Bill and Shirley. Eventually, she gave me a small nod to proceed.

"This isn't going to be pleasant, Charlie," I said, starting slowly. "For any of us. But what the heck, huh, we might as well just go ahead and put it on the table."

"I'm right in the middle of the dinner hour, Suzy," Charlie snapped. "And thanks to you guys, I'm down about ten workers at the moment. So, unless you'd like to grab an apron and wash some dishes, how about you stop wasting my time?"

"I just said I was going to put it on the table," I snapped. "Geez."

Charlie gestured for me to get on with it. I took a deep breath, exhaled loudly, and leaned forward.

"We know you killed Joshua Middleton," I said firmly.

Bill cleared his throat and gave me a small shake of his head.

"Sure, sure," I said, nodding at him. "Let me rephrase that. I know you killed him. Bill and Shirley apparently aren't quite convinced yet."

Charlie looked off into the distance with a blank expression then grinned at me.

"You think I killed Middleton?" he said, managing a chuckle. "That's rich."

"Yeah, at first, I didn't believe it either," I said. "Then when I saw you in action at our place the night you dropped by unannounced, the possibility started to work its way into my head. And once it's in there, who knows where it's going to go, right?"

"Fascinating theory, Suzy," Charlie said. "But if you remember, I was working that night."

"Yeah, you were," I said. "And I'm sure that's why you never even made the list of possible suspects. I'm also pretty sure that Bill and Shirley never even considered the possibility you might have done it. A busy restaurant kitchen, dozens of people racing around trying to keep up with all those orders. Who would even think the head chef had the time to do it? Not to mention the problem of killing him without being seen. And then getting back to work without being missed."

"Yes, all excellent points," Charlie said, smiling at me. "How indeed could I have pulled something like that off?"

"I thought you were trying to convince us," Bill said, frowning.

"Oh, he did it," I said. "The timeframe was tight, but it was definitely doable."

"I can't wait to hear this," Charlie said.

"Me too," Bill said, sitting back in his chair. "And I need to warn you, Suzy. This hotel is a national landmark and has some serious juice with a lot of politicians and other heavy hitters. Shirley and I don't need any more blowback on this case."

"Thank you, Officer," Charlie said, beaming at Bill. "You see, Suzy, even they don't believe you."

"Here's how I think it went down," I said, ignoring the naysayers. "You came in the break room, pulled that ladder down and climbed up into the storage space. If anybody had asked you why you were up there, which I'm almost positive they didn't, all you had to say was that you were getting something you needed for a recipe. And once you were up there, you made your way down the path to the other end of the storage space. Then all you needed to do was lower the ladder on that side, somehow manage to sneak up on Middleton, who was already pretty dazed and confused because he'd been punched in the face a couple of times, grab him from behind and pour the drain cleaner down his throat, then head back up the ladder. After you closed the opening in the ceiling, you made your way back down to this side, probably grabbed a can of something on the way to cover your tracks, then climbed down and closed the ladder. Someone who was familiar with the layout up there could have done the whole thing in a couple of minutes at the most."

I paused and looked around the table. Shirley sat quietly, but Bill caught my eye and gave me a quick conspiratorially wink. I knew he'd come around. Charlie sat quietly with a smirk on his face.

"Wow," Charlie said eventually. "And they call me nuts."

"The fact that you were wearing gloves eliminated the possibility of you leaving any prints at the scene," I said.

"How on earth could you possibly know I was wearing gloves that night?" Charlie said, shaking his head.

"For the same reason we saw you wearing them just a few minutes ago," I said casually.

"What?"

"We were watching you from behind the grillwork," I said. "You were making the sauce you use in your corn fritters. It's something I picked up watching Chef Claire at work. She doesn't wear gloves that often, but when she's working with fresh chilis, she always has them on to protect her hands. And I imagine that, given the way you're always cutting yourself, hot chilis on fresh cuts must be unbearably painful."

Charlie shook his head, but I could tell he was beginning to reach a slow boil.

"And I have to tell you that those fritters are amazing. They have a ton of kick to them, but the mint and yogurt you use is the perfect choice to soften the heat of the chilis."

"It's crème fraîche," Charlie said softly.

"Really? I would have sworn it was yogurt," I said, raising an eyebrow. "Well, I have to tell you, they're fantastic."

"Thanks. It's Chef Claire's recipe."

"Really? I did not know that," I said, making a mental note to ask her why she never made them.

Bill cleared his throat and I refocused.

"Sorry," I said, red-faced. "On your way back to the kitchen, you probably tossed the gloves in the trash or stuffed them in your pocket. Middleton was bleeding pretty badly, and you must have had some of it on your gloves. And your uniform. But since you're always cutting yourself, if your staff did happen to see some blood on your uniform, it probably didn't even register with them."

"A fascinating theory, Suzy," Charlie said, slowly clenching and unclenching his fingers. "Truly remarkable." Then he glanced around the table with a smile that transitioned into a sneer. "And, of course, you have proof, right?"

"No, not yet, I'm afraid," I said, then glanced at Bill and Shirley. "Unless you guys have been holding out on me."

"No," Shirley said, shaking her head. "We got nothing."

228

"There you go," Charlie said. "No fingerprints, no blood. Not to mention one other important fact. What motive could I possibly have to kill him?"

"Oh, the motive was easy," I said. "As soon as your sister told you that all the banks had turned her down for the loan and you saw how devastated she was, I'm sure you went straight into protective brother mode. And I've witnessed first-hand what that looks like."

"Why would I blame Middleton for Bobbie not getting her loan?" Charlie said, taunting me.

"Actually, it wouldn't have taken a smart guy like you long to figure it out," I said, shrugging. "Once I figured out how some of the facts were connected, I put it together in a couple of hours."

Charlie flinched but said nothing.

"That's my theory," I said. "Well, that's most of it anyway."

"But still no proof," Charlie said. "Too bad about that, huh?"

"I said we didn't have any proof, *yet*," I said, giving him a small smile.

"No witnesses, no fingerprints, no blood," he said, shaking his head. "I hate to say it, Suzy, but I don't like your chances."

"He has a point," Bill said, glancing at Charlie before slipping me another wink.

"There you go," Charlie said. "Even the cops think you're nuts."

"Oh, there's blood," I said, nodding. "Maybe not a lot of it, but these guys don't need much to build a case."

"That's true," Bill said.

"Blood? Where would there be any blood?" Charlie said, sitting a bit more upright in his chair.

"On your uniform," I said, shrugging.

Charlie laughed. I waited it out.

"My uniform?" he said. "You own a restaurant so you should know that kitchen staff uniforms are washed on a regular basis. Even if there had been blood on my uniform, which there wasn't, it's long gone by now."

"Oh, I doubt it, Charlie," I said, shaking my head. "Chef Claire has several uniforms she uses in rotation until they wear out. And while they are being washed on a regular basis, the uniform you were wearing the night Middleton got killed couldn't have been washed more than once or twice since then."

"So what?"

"This is the part where I need to defer to the experts. They know a lot more about forensics than I do."

Bill sat forward in his chair and grinned at me.

"I thought you were joking earlier when you said you might need me to explain how different bleaches work," he said.

"I know you did," I said, smiling back at him. "Smooth transition, huh?"

"Yeah, not bad."

"As much as I'm enjoying your good-cop, crazy-lady routine, can we please get on with this? I have to get back to work to see if there's any chance I can salvage this night."

"That's the least of your problems, Charlie," Bill said evenly as he looked at the chef. "What Suzy is talking about is the difference between chlorine-based versus oxygen bleaches. Both remove bloodstains as far as the naked eye is concerned, but fortunately for people like me, forensics experts can use chemicals like luminol or phenolphthalein to show where blood is still present. Unless an oxygen bleach was used. That's much better at removing all traces of blood residue. But if a *chlorine* bleach was used to wash the garment in question, it could have been cleaned a dozen times, and those chemicals could still reveal the presence of blood."

"Maybe the hotel uses an oxygen bleach," Charlie said, tight-lipped.

"Highly unlikely," I said. "Oxygen bleaches tend to be more expensive than chlorine. And as I'm sure I don't have to tell you, in the restaurant business, every dollar counts."

"It's too bad I don't have a saw with me," Charlie said, laughing. "It would be so easy to cut that limb you've climbed out to the edge of. This is absolutely insane. And you're forgetting the most important piece of information."

"I know," I said as a sad frown formed on my face.

"What do you mean, you know?"

"Never mind," I said, suddenly fatigued as my adrenaline level dropped. "Please, continue."

"If I was working that night, something that at least twenty people in the kitchen alone can confirm, how did I know that Middleton was in that storage room?"

I exhaled and felt the tears begin to form in my eyes.

"Because you had help," I whispered.

Charlie flinched, and I noticed when he gripped the edge of the table hard with both hands. Bill also noticed and I saw him unsnap his holster. I snuck a quick glance at the large object inside the holster and recognized the taser. At least I hoped it was a taser. If it were a handgun, it was big enough to blow a hole the size of a basketball through somebody.

"Bobbie helped you," I said, sniffling.

"My sister helped me kill Middleton?" Charlie said, forcing a manic chuckle, hunched in his chair like he was about to pounce on me.

"She wasn't involved in the killing," I said softly. "But she either called you or sent you a text to let you know Middleton had walked into that storage room. Unfortunately for both of you, that's going to be very easy to confirm."

"Why on earth would Bobbie agree to do that? She doesn't have a malicious bone in her body," Charlie said, trying to hang on for dear life.

"Because she's scared to death to say no to you," I whispered. "You almost pulled her arm out of its socket the other night just because she didn't tell you she was coming to see us. Who knows what you would have done to her if she refused your demand about helping you take Middleton out?"

Charlie sat quietly for several seconds, then clamored out of his chair and pushed Bill by the shoulders. Bill toppled over in his chair, and I heard his flashlight and the taser bounce across the floor. Charlie dashed for the door, stepped on the flashlight and lost his footing. I was reminded of a Saturday morning cartoon when he windmilled his arms to help him catch his balance as he went airborne, then fell on his butt with a thud. Then he quickly recovered and made another beeline for the door. I climbed over Bill who was groaning as he struggled to get to his feet and grabbed the taser off the floor. I knelt down on one knee and pointed it with both hands at Charlie's back.

"Don't make me use this, Charlie. You remember what happened the other night."

"Hah, nice try, crazy lady," he said with a mocking tone as he glanced over his shoulder. "You don't have a chance of hitting-"

I was amazed when I realized that not only had I managed to fire the weapon, I'd actually hit him. An electrode was protruding from both of his thighs, right below a very tender region of the male physique, and he was soon on the floor spasming. Then a puddle began to form underneath his legs.

"Wow. That's gotta hurt," I said softly through a grimace.

"Nice shot," Shirley said, patting me on the back.

"He probably should have tried to swerve," I said, deflecting. "It was a pretty easy shot. All I had to do was point and pull the trigger."

Bill got to his feet, removed a pair of handcuffs from his belt as he stepped around the puddle, and secured Charlie's hands behind his back. We continued to stare at the spasming chef sprawled face down on the kitchen floor.

"Shouldn't we remove the electrodes?" Shirley said eventually.

"Nah," Bill said, enjoying the show. "Let's give it a minute."

I watched Charlie progress through another energetic round of groans and twitches.

"Good call."

Chapter 22

Shirley called the command desk to report in and request backup. To minimize embarrassment to the hotel, she asked that all assigned personnel use the service entrance off the back of the kitchen. I watched Bill help Charlie to his feet, lead him back into the center of the kitchen, then handcuff one of his legs to a steam table that was anchored into the floor. Bill quietly read Charlie his rights, a set of short statements very similar to the version we used on our side of the border.

Then the hotel manager stormed into the kitchen screaming for Charlie. Apparently, he'd been receiving a lot of complaints from both customers and the serving staff about how long it was taking for the soup course to arrive. He glared at Charlie and was about to give him an earful when he noticed the two sets of handcuffs he was wearing. Bewildered, he looked around the kitchen and frowned.

"What's going on? Where the heck is everybody?" the manager said.

"Running for the hills, I think," I said, spying an order of corn fritters sitting under a set of warming lights.

"What?"

"Nothing," I said, shaking my head as I reached for the fritters.

Bill led the manager to one side and had a short conversation with him out of earshot. Judging from the manager's reaction, Bill didn't spare any details. The manager approached Charlie, cursed him out, then glanced around the kitchen again.

"What the heck am I going to do now?" the manager said to no one in particular.

"I imagine you're going to have to close the kitchen," I said, extending the small plate I was holding. "Fritter?"

"No, thanks," he said, shaking his head. "They're way too spicy for me." He exhaled loudly, took another long look around, then nodded. "Yeah, that's what I'm going to have to do." He glared at Charlie one last time then left the kitchen as fast as his legs could carry him.

Bill seemed interested in what I was holding, and I approached with the plate of fritters extended.

"How hot are they?" he said, glancing warily at the plate.

"Not bad," I said, chewing.

He selected one, took a bite, then spit it into a napkin.

"You set me up," he said, wiping his mouth. "How on earth can you eat something that spicy?"

"With lots of practice," I said, grinning at him.

He leaned against one of the stainless steel tables and rubbed his forehead.

"Man, I'm tired. It's been a long week," he said, then focused on me. "I really need to thank you. That was an amazing piece of work. I can't believe you put all that together."

"I just got lucky," I said, deflecting once again. "You guys would have figured it out."

"Yeah, probably. Maybe," he said, tentatively. "As soon as our backup gets here, we'll go grab the sister."

"Yeah, it has to be done," I said softly as a wave of sadness washed over me. "You won't mind if I don't tag along?"

"You had enough for one day?"

"Yeah, I can only handle so much disappointment before the waterworks start flowing," I said, giving him a sad smile.

"It's too bad," he said, shaking his head. "Just when her ship is about to finally come in, she gets involved in something like that."

"He's going away for a very long time, right?" I said, nodding at Charlie who continued to stand quietly staring down at the floor, chained to the steam table.

"For killing the CEO of a major corporation in a national landmark hotel?" Bill said, chuckling. "Yeah, I have a feeling they'll be a lot of people wanting to make an example of Charlie. I'm sure they're gonna hit him with first-degree murder. That carries a life sentence, but if he behaves himself and is the model prisoner, he might be eligible for parole in twenty-five years. That's the best he can hope for. Unless he doesn't confess and we don't find any blood."

"You'll find it," I said, nodding.

"Yeah, I'm betting on it," he said. "And if he treated his sister half as bad as you say he did, I'm pretty sure she'll end up rolling over on him. It might be the only way to save her own skin."

"What's going to happen to Bobbie?" I said, then felt the tears beginning to form.

"That's a harder question," he said, shrugging. "If she also gets tagged with murder one, she's looking at the same sentence as her brother. If she cooperates, gets the right lawyer, blah, blah, blah, you know the drill, she might get a lesser charge. But at a minimum, I'd say she's looking at five to seven years before she's parole eligible."

"Geez, that's a long time to be locked up," I said, exhaling loudly.

"Yeah," Bill said. "And if I were you, I'd start looking for another CEO to run your dog toy company."

I nodded as I noticed Shirley coming in through the back door and heading toward us. She gave Charlie a wide berth as she walked past him and came to a stop next to us.

"Okay, we've got six officers here and another half dozen on the way," she said, glancing around.

"A dozen?" Bill said, laughing. "For a solved case that includes the murderer handcuffed to a steam table?"

"I know, it's crazy, huh?" she said, shaking her head. "But half the cops are going to be assigned to keep the media jackals at bay. It just broke on the news, and the chief is already getting calls from all sorts of our favorite government officials."

"Then this is the perfect time for us to get out of here and go arrest the sister," Bill said.

"Great minds think alike. Do you want to ride along, Suzy?" Shirley said. "It's the least we can do. You know, for closure and all that."

"No, thanks. I'm going to head home," I said, extending the plate to her. "Fritter?"

"Thanks," she said, popping one of the deep-fried gems into her mouth. Then she nodded. "These are fantastic."

Bill gave his partner a look of amazement when Shirley grabbed another off the plate. She swallowed it, gave me a hug, then gestured at him.

"Let's go, Mr. Magic," she said.

"Mr. Magic?" I said, raising an eyebrow.

"I needed a nickname for him. Since we're going to be together as long as he's still able to take a breath. It was getting old just calling him Bill."

"The only time she calls me by my name lately is when she's mad," Bill said, glancing around to make sure no one was watching before giving her a quick kiss.

I shook hands with both of them and watched them leave through the back door. I checked my watch, felt a hunger pang, and wondered if I should stop for dinner on my way home. Then I remembered where I was.

"Duh," I said, heading to the chef station.

I found a crispy baguette, sliced it in half, then split it down the middle. I rummaged through one of the fridges and grabbed a selection of deli meats, cheeses, pickles, grilled onions, and a large tomato. I constructed my own version of a Dagwood sandwich, then searched the area around me. Unable to locate what I was looking for, I glanced over at Charlie who was still staring off into space.

"Hey, Charlie."

"What?"

"Where do you keep the mayonnaise?"

"What are you making?" he said, glancing over.

"Just a Dagwood."

"Skip the mayo and go with the garlic-dill remoulade," he said. "It's in the mini-fridge just to your left."

"Cool," I said, grabbing the container and slathering on a heavy dose. "Thanks."

"No problem," he said, then stared off at nothing in particular.

I cut the massive sandwich into manageable pieces, then wrapped the monster and slid it into my bag. I slung my bag over my shoulder and walked over to him.

"I'm so sorry, Charlie. Not that it matters much, huh?"

"No, it doesn't," he said, making eye contact. "Did I hear that cop mention a minimum of twenty-five years?"

"Yeah," I whispered.

"Maybe they'll give me a job in the kitchen," he said to himself.

"Maybe."

Given his anger issues and expertise with knives, I had my doubts. But I kept them to myself as I headed toward the door. Then I stopped and turned around.

"Take care of yourself, Charlie."

"A little late for that," he said, shrugging. "Tell her I said goodbye, okay?"

"I'll do that."

I gave him a small wave, left the kitchen, and headed for the lobby. I went outside through the revolving door and fished around in my bag for my parking ticket. The same attendant who'd met me earlier approached.

"How did your meeting go?"

"It was eventful."

"Did you have anything to do with all the cops showing up?"

"Nah," I said, shaking my head. "I'm not sure what's going on with that."

"Yeah, me neither," he said, accepting my ticket. "But we're always the last ones to know. I'll be right back."

He trotted off, and I walked down the steps to wait for my car. I buttoned my coat to fend off the cold, but the wind was down, and the sky had cleared. I glanced up at the moon and stars and took a deep breath and felt the cold air hit my lungs. I took a step back when my car arrived, and the attendant hopped out and left the door open. I handed him a twenty, and he glanced at it then grinned at me.

"Twenty bucks?"

"You mentioned something about making twenty bucks earlier. I guess it stuck with me."

"Thanks," he said as he toed the pavement with the tip of his shoe. "Look, I was wondering if you get up here often."

"Yeah, from time to time," I said. "And I imagine I might be coming more often in the future."

"Would you be interested in maybe going out sometime? You know, dinner and a movie. Or if you're up for it, we could hit a club or two."

I smiled at him as I thought about it. Then I flashed back to Bill and Shirley and how happy they seemed to be. And the more I thought about it, I decided that happy didn't really capture it. They were content. Fully committed to each other and at peace with the idea. And I hoped they'd be able to stay that way. I studied the attendant's face. He was younger than I, but not too young. And he was certainly attractive in a boyish sort of way I found appealing.

"You mentioned earlier that you're trying to make it as a stand-up comic," I said.

"Yes, I am."

"Are you any good at it?"

"Yeah, I think I am," he said without boasting.

242

"Then that means you'll eventually start making the rounds of all the comedy clubs, right?"

"You gotta go where the work is," he said, shrugging.

"And you'd be on the road constantly, right?"

"Most of the year, I'm sure," he said, nodding.

"Then I have to say, while I'm tempted to say yes, I'm afraid it's going to be a no. I'm sorry."

"Just because there's a chance at some point in the future we wouldn't see each other very often?"

"Pretty much," I said, smiling and nodding.

"Hey, it's not like I'm looking for anything serious," he said, frowning.

"Yeah, I know," I said, gently placing a hand on his cheek. "But I am."

I gave him a hug, climbed into my car and left him standing there with a confused look on his face. I waved goodbye through the rear-view mirror, grabbed my phone from my bag and slid it into its dashboard holder. I set the sandwich on the passenger seat then called Josie and put the phone on speaker.

"Hey," she said. "We were beginning to worry. Is everything okay?"

"Yeah, it's fine," I said, reaching for one of the pieces of the Dagwood. "I just left, and I'm on my way home. Is Chef Claire there?"

"Yeah, she took the night off."

"Good for her," I said, taking a bite of sandwich. "Put me on speaker."

"Hi, Suzy," Chef Claire said. "Any news?"

"Yeah, you could say that," I said, giving up trying to eat and talk at the same time. I set the piece of sandwich on the passenger seat next to the rest of its family as I kept an eye out for signs to the highway.

Then I launched into the story of how I'd spent my day. A roller coaster day filled with twists and turns, emotional highs and lows, and enough mood swings to empty a shrink's prescription pad. When I got to the part of Charlie's arrest for the murder of Joshua Middleton, I waited for Chef Claire's reaction when she heard the news. All I got was a long silence.

"Chef Claire?"

"Yeah?"

"Are you okay?"

"I think so. Part of me feels incredibly sad. And I feel awful about what might happen to Bobbie. But I'd be lying if I didn't say I'm also relieved. I can finally stop worrying about him doing something like that to me."

"Yeah, I get that," I said, working the car into the right lane and onto the entrance ramp to the highway. "What are you guys doing?"

"Just waiting for you," Josie said. "We thought we'd catch up, play with the dogs, drink some wine, maybe watch a movie. You know, the usual."

"Perfect."

"Are you going to be hungry?" Chef Claire said.

I glanced over at the passenger seat at the sandwich that was big enough to warrant its own seatbelt.

"Geez, I sure hope not," I said.

"What?"

"Nothing."

"Okay, we'll see you in a couple of hours," Josie said. "Drive safe."

"Will do."

I ended the call and reached for a piece of the sandwich. I drove with one eye on the highway and the other on the sandwich as I tried to figure out a way to eat without losing half of it on the floor. Traffic was light, and I set the cruise control to sixty-five. My kitchen creation was delicious, and I savored every bite.

I was glad I took Charlie's suggestion to stay away from the mayonnaise.

The man may have been a deranged killer, but he sure knew his remoulade.

Epilogue

Charlie was officially charged with the murder of Joshua Middleton before I even made it home. When convicted, as everyone associated with the case is certain he will be, Charlie will be looking at a mandatory life sentence. And as Bill had said, if he's a really good boy and proves he can play well with others in the same sandbox, parole after the mandatory twenty-five is a possibility, however remote. The certainty of his conviction was pretty much signed, sealed, and delivered when Bobbie, as Bill had suggested she might, confessed to her complicity in the murder and made it perfectly clear to anyone who would listen that she only agreed to help her brother out because she feared for her life. It wasn't much of a defense, but it was probably the best option she had.

As soon as Bobbie rolled over on her brother, Charlie's lawyer briefly considered an insanity plea. But that was scrapped when the judge who caught the case, a devoted foodie with a fondness for pheasant and elk who'd eaten Charlie's food several times in the past, rejected the lawyer's appeal on the grounds that anybody who could work that kind of magic on wild game couldn't possibly be considered clinically insane. When the lawyer tried to challenge the judge's ruling as being arbitrary and capricious, the judge sent him back to his seat with a thinly veiled threat to eat the man's liver with some fava beans and a six-pack of Molson. The lawyer, who apparently also moonlights as a literary agent, soon changed his strategy and is currently in negotiations with a major publishing house about a combination biography-cookbook about Charlie's life and some of his favorite recipes, tentatively titled: *Three Hots and a Cot*. Chef Claire has already gotten word to the lawyer that, if any of her recipes end up in the book, she's going to grab her bat and pay him a little visit.

Bobbie, whose tenure as the CEO of Wags was over before the ink had time to dry on the contract, is still hopeful that she'll be able to avoid a lengthy stretch of prison time. The word on the street is that she'll be incredibly lucky if she only gets seven years. If she gets five or less, Shirley says Bobbie should immediately buy all the lotto tickets she can get her hands on.

Bobbie was the subject of constant discussion and debate between the three of us for weeks, especially around the topic of what we were going to do about the dog toy company. We strongly considered just walking away from the whole thing given everything else we had on our plate, but we kept coming back to the nagging thought that the idea was simply too good to pass up. In the end, we agreed to move forward, especially after my mother had, in no uncertain terms, questioned our sanity.

From a personal perspective, all three of us were torn when it came to Bobbie. We felt bad for her and knew that her fear of

Charlie had forced her to do things she would never choose to do without her brother's pressure. But we had a hard time getting past the idea that she had lied to us, not to mention the fact that she had also played an active role in a murder.

That most certainly didn't help assuage our concerns.

We debated at length additional reasons that might have driven her actions. During those debates, every tired theory and pop-culture cliché we could remember were put on the table, kicked back and forth, and beat to death: Nature versus nurture, rational choice, victimization and the social conflict theory, punishment versus compassion, chicken and the egg, and society's impact on individual responsibility, which, late one night after too much wine, laughingly morphed into the dog ate my homework theory of personal responsibility.

We decided to visit Bobby after she made bail. Once we got past a very awkward first half-hour, we were able to move forward and negotiate a new ownership deal. The three of us ended up keeping sixty percent of the company and gave twenty percent to Bobbie, which she was stunned and delighted to receive. After all, we decided, it was her idea, and she should share some of the profits. And as Josie pointed out on the drive home, unless the price of prison-cigarettes and pruno continued to skyrocket, Bobbie should be able to save pretty much everything she made while she was away and have quite a nest egg by the time she got out.

Given the stark reality behind Josie's black humor, I probably laughed harder than I should have and almost drove off the road doing seventy.

We weren't quite sure what to do with the remaining twenty percent but were committed to making that decision before we headed off to the Caymans. We decided to use one of our family dinner nights to get it done, and over a Beef Wellington that Chef Claire surprised us with out of the blue, we kicked around a variety of ideas about how to allocate the remaining ownership stake. My mother, who'd been listening quietly to our conversation, started making notes as she ate. Then she put her utensils down and proceeded to outline her list of thirteen suggestions for jumpstarting and taking the company to the next level. We listened in stunned silence, and when she finished, she went back to work on her Beef Wellington. The three of us looked at each other, nodded in unison, then welcomed my mother aboard.

And as long as the three of us stick together, our sixty percent ownership stake should help us maintain at least some semblance of control.

Our search for a new CEO continues. It's a crucial decision, and it's probably going to be a long process, but I'm doing my best not to obsess over it. However, we were able to make one hire I feel really good about. I kept my own promise to make it up to Marjorie's son, Thomas, the young man I'd added to my initial list of suspects on the night Middleton was killed. Thomas is Wags' new Head of Logistics and is currently scouring Ottawa for warehouse space that can be converted into a manufacturing facility. I saw him recently, and he pointed out the downtown penthouse condo he's renting as we drove around the city in his new sports car.

I'm pretty sure he's forgiven me.

Apart from that, life around the Inn has fallen back into its predictable early winter pattern. Sammy and Jill are excited about running the place for the entire winter, and we're looking forward to spending ours in the sun and sand. Jill finally convinced us that she'd be able to handle running the rescue program in addition to her regular duties so we gave her the job. And the other night, Josie and I did our final review and realized that everything was done, and we could head off with a clear conscience and not have to worry about the Inn or the welfare of the dogs while we were gone.

The weather is getting colder by the day, and the dogs are getting increasingly resistant to spending any more time outside than is necessary. Given the half-foot of snow and the blustery wind out of the north we dealt with yesterday, it's hard to argue with their logic. As for Jack, he's become a full-fledged member of the family, and we've already turned down several adoption requests. At some point, we'll probably consider one of them, but he's doing well, gets along great with all the other dogs, and has a personality that never ceases to put a smile on our face. I suppose that someday the perfect family will come through the front door and we'll be more than happy to let him go.

Maybe.

Thanksgiving was wonderful, and we shared it with a collection of friends and their dogs I couldn't have dreamed possible when I was younger. We counted our blessings then, over turkey sandwiches around midnight, began to count the days. And since we'd reluctantly agreed to my mother's request to spend Christmas at her house in the Caymans, we found ourselves at a small airstrip just outside of town on the morning of the 23rd shaking our heads at the four dogs who were slowly making their way up the stairs onto the private jet we'd chartered. Chloe led the way, paused on the top step to glance back and make sure the others were following, then stepped inside. Al and Dente bounded past Chef Claire, closely followed by Captain. We waited until our luggage and the dog crates were loaded then headed up the stairs. We got the dogs into their crates for takeoff, ignored the stink-eyes all four were giving us, then took our seats. Josie and Chef Claire sat in the row behind me and kept their distance when they saw my look of fear and panic begin to set in. I focused on my breathing and buckled in tight. As we waited for the pilot to finish his pre-flight, my phone buzzed. I glanced at the number and answered in the middle of the second ring.

"Victor Rollins," I said, elated to have something to take my mind off takeoff. "I was wondering when we were going to hear from you."

"Yeah, sorry about that," he said, obviously in a very good mood. "I wanted to wait until I had something definite to tell you."

"And?"

"I got good news and even better news," he said, laughing. "Which do you want first?"

"Your call, Victor. Surprise me."

"I just got the CEO job," he said, then rattled his ice cubes.

I ignored the annoying rattle.

"Congratulations. It sure took them long enough to make up their minds."

"Yeah, Wendell was squawking about it, but then he suddenly quieted down after a couple of board members let him know they'd heard some disturbing rumors about what he and Middleton had been up to."

"Really?"

"You wouldn't know anything about that, would you, Suzy?"

"Me? Victor, I'm shocked that you would even think such a thing."

One row back, Josie snorted loudly.

"Well, anyway, I'm in, and Wendell is on a very short leash," Rollins said, again rattling his ice near the phone.

"I know what you're doing, Victor," I snapped. "Knock it off."

"You're so easy to get a rise out of," he said, laughing. "Now for the other good news. What would you guys say to a ten-year deal?"

"You want a ten-year agreement?" I said, surprised. We'd been hoping to possibly get one for five. "That's pretty unusual, isn't it?"

"Maybe a little," he said. "But we think this thing is going to go big and go big in a hurry. And we're willing to agree to ten years just so we don't lose any momentum down the road by having to waste a lot of time negotiating a new deal."

"You mean you want to lock us up now and not have to worry about giving us any more money until you absolutely have to, right?"

"Nothing gets past you."

I turned around in my seat to look at Josie and Chef Claire who were listening to the conversation.

"Did you guys get that?" I said to them.

They both nodded and gave me thumbs up.

"Okay, Victor. Ten years it is. But we'll want to include a walk-away provision after five in case either of us wants to get out."

"C'mon, Suzy," he said, rattling his ice. "Why on earth would you want to walk away?"

"Add it to the list and let the lawyers hash it out," I said, not in the mood to argue with him.

"Will do," he said, his good mood apparently unshakeable. "Any update on your side?"

"Yeah, we're still looking for the new CEO, but we just hired our Head of Logistics. He's a good kid. You'll like him. At the moment, he's scouting locations in Ottawa for the manufacturing facility."

"Manufacturing?"

"The toys aren't going to make themselves, Victor."

"No, of course not," he said, confused. "But why would you do that? I thought you'd be subbing that out and having the toys built in China."

"No, that's not going to happen," I said firmly.

"Why on earth not?"

"Because they eat dogs in China."

"Oh, yeah," he said after a long pause. "I forgot who I was dealing with for a moment. Well, have it your way. It's your company. But it's going to cut into your margins."

"I'm sure it will. But that point is non-negotiable," I said, glancing over my shoulder and receiving nods of approval from Josie and Chef Claire. "Besides, we like the idea of providing some jobs to folks on both sides of the border." I decided to throw him a changeup. "How's Wilma?"

"She's great," he said. "I moved in with her. But her apartment is pretty small, so I imagine we'll start looking at houses pretty soon. You know, now that I got the job."

"Good for you," I said, nodding. Time to see if he could hit a fastball. "How's your drinking?"

"What?"

"Well, the last few times we talked, it seemed like you were hitting the scotch pretty hard."

"That was just a temporary stage I was going through to help me cope with all the stress Middleton was putting me through."

"Whatever you say, Victor."

"You sound just like Wilma."

"Good. You should listen to her. What's the deal with her idea for the pet massage business?"

"That's on hold for the moment," he said. "We agreed to wait and see what happens with our relationship before we do anything with it."

"Got it," I said, leaning back in my seat as the plane started to roll down the runway.

I took a few deeps breaths when we left the ground and quickly ascended. Neither one of us said anything for a long time. I assumed he was refilling his drink. I, on the other hand, was waiting for my stomach to get off my vocal chords.

"I'd like to thank you again, Suzy," he said. "You didn't have to do that. In fact, I'm still not sure why you did."

"Self-interest, primarily," I said, unfastening my seat belt as the plane leveled off without the slightest sign of turbulence. "You're going to make us a lot of money."

"We're going to make each other a lot of money, Suzy. But I don't think that's the reason you did it."

"I can't wait to hear your theories, Victor," I said, getting up from my seat to open the dog crates. "But not today. In fact, I think I'm about to lose the connection."

"Okay, I'll be in touch soon. Enjoy the Caymans," he said, giving his ice one last loud rattle then laughing as he hung up.

I put my phone away, returned to my seat and made room for Chloe on my lap. She stretched out and rolled over on her back. I gently scratched her belly and moved my seat back.

"Do you think we're going to be able to work with him?" Josie said, leaning forward from the seat behind me.

"Oh, we're not going to have to work with him," I said, closing my eyes.

"You're going to turn your mother loose on him, aren't you?"

"Yup," I said with an evil grin.

"That's diabolical," Chef Claire said, laughing.

"Anything to get away from that incessant rattling of ice cubes," I said. "It's so annoying."

Josie rattled the ice cubes in her glass of soda in my ear.

"You mean, like this?" she deadpanned.

"You're really not funny."

"Time will tell," she said, giving the ice another rattle in my ear.

"Chef Claire, please do something," I said, trying to drift off for a nap.

"You mean, other than laugh?"

"Break out the brownies. That oughta shut her up."